I0731803

THE MYSTERY OF RUBY'S MASK

ROSE DONOVAN

MOON SNAIL PRESS

MORE RUBY DOVE MYSTERIES

Join my reader group! Details can be found at the end of *The Mystery of Ruby's Mask.*

Cast of Characters at the Villa Potenza

Ruby Dove – Student of chemistry at Oxford, fashion designer and amateur spy-sleuth. On a mission to enliven a masked ball.

Fina Aubrey-Havelock – Student of history at Oxford, assistant seamstress to Ruby, and her best friend. Feeling like a second fiddle at this weekend party.

Pixley Hayford – A shameless journalist on the hunt for a scoop. Always game for a Ruby and Fina adventure, though this one is definitely more than he bargained for.

Sergio Chapman – Cambridge law professor with a roving eye.

Marchesa Gloria Della Corsini – American-born marquise. Owner of the villa and a bit of a queen. Drama, that is.

Emil Pleischner – Swiss secretary to Lord Mayhew. A sweet man, and a talker.

Lloyd Mayhew – English MP with heart trouble.

Marilyn Asher – American-born British MP. Childhood friend of Marchesa Gloria.

Madam Zora – Ukrainian fashion designer and lover of witches.

Hazel Padmore – Secretary to exiled Ethiopian empress living in London. Possible rival to Ruby.

Il Grande Vittorio – Magician with a shark-like smile.

Isa Ficre – Vittorio's contortionist assistant.

Daria Lazzari – Maid at the villa.

Gustavo Pavoni – Butler at the villa.

Iveta Da Silva – Precious stones expert. A force of nature and a good friend to Ruby. Loves gems of all sorts.

Salvo Giudici – Local commissario with a love of opera and a positive attitude toward life.

Enrico Moretti – Bright young assistant to Giudici. Does not approve of his chief's light-hearted attitude.

Puffy – Villa Potenza's cat. Only Fina seems interested in the feline.

1

Fog swirled around Fina's legs.

The fingers of mist crawled higher, up to her waist.

A mourning dove cooed across the lake.

Footsteps tapped toward her.

Where was blasted Pixley? He was due on shore over an hour ago. Perhaps the fog had stopped the ferry running from Bellagio to Varenna.

The footsteps drew closer. She spun round, blinked, and stood still, too afraid to move lest she fell into Lake Como.

"May I help you?"

Fina waved furiously, but the fog only swirled around her hand, growing ever more opaque.

She spied a figure ambling toward her with a lazy step. He stopped, less than a foot away. Though the breach of personal space was alarming, Fina was grateful that anyone should rise out of the fog. The man's homburg half-covered a wicked, crooked grin, and a long, thin nose. Clad in a green travelling suit with a blue tie, he resembled a Rudolph Valentino with curly hair.

"Pleased to meet you. I'm Sergio Chapman."

"I'm Fina Aubrey-Havelock." He encircled the whole of her hand and shook it. She drew back, stomach clenched.

"You're probably wondering why I'm called Sergio Chapman."

Fina looked over his shoulder. She was more concerned by his peculiar behaviour.

"My mother is English and my father is Italian."

"Well, my mother's Irish and my father's English." She paused. "As fascinating as family history might be, could you tell me when the ferry's due to arrive? And where is the dock? The cursed fog blocks everything."

Sergio lit a cigarette, adding to the air pollution. "This has happened before. They hold the ferry until the fog lifts."

As soon as he spoke, the fog began to thin, revealing a blue Lake Como, surrounded by snow-capped mountains.

"What did I tell you?" Sergio pointed his cigarette at a peninsula in the distance. "There's Bellagio and the ferry. We'll be there in a tick."

Ignoring the splendour around her, Fina peered at Sergio. Though he was no more than thirty, the corners of his brown eyes crinkled when he smiled, adding years to his face.

He puffed his cigarette. "Are you on holiday? Odd season for a toddle to Como."

"Then why are you here?" said Fina, determined not to be rattled.

"Feisty, aren't you? I'm travelling to the Villa Potenza – Marchesa Gloria Della Corsini's place. My wretched secretary was supposed to fetch me hours ago, though the fog must have prevented it."

Before Fina could tell him she was also a guest at Villa Potenza, a chattering crowd spontaneously formed around them at the dock. A dapper uniformed man, with a cap and large silver moustache, held up his hand. "*Silencio*. Tickets, please!"

Fina clutched her ticket as she scanned the ferry dock for Pixley. His bald, round head and impeccable clothes usually made him easy to spot. But no one amidst the pale white passengers remotely resembled her friend.

"My secretary isn't here. Well, I'd better board anyway." Sergio offered her a hooked arm. "Are you coming?"

Fina stood still.

A noticeboard, flapping with paper, drew her attention.

On the paper was a sketch, and under the sketch, the word *criminale.*

An unmistakeable bald head.

Pixley Hayford.

Fina snatched the drawing and stuffed it into her pocket.

Sergio's eyes narrowed. "I say, was that something interesting?"

"No, nothing," mumbled Fina. Heart thumping, she kept her eyes down and away from Sergio. She inhaled cold, fresh air. "I'm also staying at Villa Potenza. Are you friends with Marchesa Della Corsini?"

Sergio's eyes wrinkled in amusement. "Glad you'll be joining us." He held out an arm as Fina boarded the ferry ramp. "The marchesa didn't invite me directly. A friend of a friend, shall we say. She's—"

Silence. Fina turned around.

Sergio had vanished.

A splashing noise echoed across the quiet lake.

"Man overboard!" she screamed.

Sergio thrashed about, unable to swim.

Fina shut her eyes. Sergio was caught between the ferry and the dock.

Passengers rushed to one side, pointing and yelling. Under the weight of the onlookers, the ferry edged closer to the dock. If Sergio didn't drown, he might be crushed.

The ferry steward threw off his cap and jumped up and down. *"Questa è un'emergenza!"*

A man in a brown suit threw off his fedora and jacket and plunged into the icy water.

The steward yelled and waved at the passengers.

The ferry slowly rocked backward, away from Sergio.

Fina sighed.

The man in the brown suit grabbed Sergio and dragged him toward the ramp. A ferry attendant threw down a looped rope. Inch by inch, the pair were hoisted up to the dock, where they collapsed on the ramp, spluttering and coughing.

A woman passenger scurried down the ramp with an armload of blankets. She wrapped the men in them.

The steward nodded at the captain. The captain nodded back, and returned to the helm.

"Wait!" croaked the man in the brown suit. "I must board. Let us get on."

Stroking his moustache, the steward shrugged. Sergio and the rescuer limped on board.

Fina rushed to Sergio's side. "What happened?"

Sergio spit out more water and jiggled his ear. "Someone pushed me. I didn't see who."

"But why?"

"Haven't a blessed clue. One minute, I was telling you I was invited by Lord Mayhew's secretary, Emil Pleischner, and the next I was in the water."

Fina leaned against the railing as the boat lurched forward. She stared at the breathtaking mountain vista and colourful houses of Varenna they were leaving behind. Why was Sergio lying? She swore he'd said "She's" before he was pushed over. But now Sergio was claiming a man had invited him. She shivered. Too many murder cases would make one suspicious of everyone and everything. Though the Pixley drawing was troubling. She'd ask him about it when she arrived.

Fina opened her capacious bag and lifted out a thermos. She poured strong, sweet tea into the lid and handed it to Sergio.

"Splendid. Thank you so much." He lifted the cup to his lips, as if it were the holy grail. "Ah. Much better. Now, you were about to tell me who invited you to Villa Potenza."

"It's complicated."

"We have another ten minutes until we arrive. Besides, a story will distract me from my wet clothes. It's dashed cold."

"I'm an assistant to a dress designer. Her name is Ruby Dove. She was invited by the marchesa to design a costume for her masked ball on Mardi Gras."

"And where is this famous Miss Dove?"

"We're both students at Oxford. I convinced my tutor to let me take my schoolwork for two weeks so I don't fall behind. Ruby was not so fortunate – she's reading chemistry – so she had to stay on. She'll arrive this afternoon."

"Why didn't you wait for her?"

"She insisted I take measurements and ask for the marchesa's ideas. My train was held up in Bergamo, so I won't make much progress."

Sergio took another sip. "So you're a student at Oxford. Interesting."

"Why?"

"Because I'm a professor at Cambridge. A professor of law."

Fina's body stiffened, as if she were a soldier who'd discovered she was in the company of a general. "Oh, Professor Chapman, why didn't you say so?"

He chuckled. "See? Your posture transformed as soon as I told you. It's better to keep it under wraps most of the time. People have a lot of expectations of you – perhaps they remember a terrifying teacher and project it onto you, as dear Dr Freud would say."

Fina softened. "I can imagine. But it must be awfully useful when you need authority."

"That it is, that it is." He gazed at the mountains.

Fina gasped as Bellagio came into view. The sun filtered through the clouds, casting a yellow glow against the buildings with red roofs and lush green hedges. "It's gorgeous!" she cried.

Sergio gave her his crooked smile. "Don't let it deceive you. It's a mass of intrigue, betrayal, and drama."

He pointed at the dock. "Look. There's my secretary."

Mr Pixley Hayford grinned and waved at them.

2

The ferry lurched toward the dock, squealing and screeching. Fina grasped the railing but it turned out to be Sergio's arm.

"Oh, pardon me. So sorry."

"No trouble at all." He grinned as he let the blankets slide off him onto the deck. Fina crouched down and began folding them.

"Leave them," he said. "Let the crew clean them up."

Fina thought this was rude, but didn't say so. She was keen to stay on the good side of this man, not because she liked him, but because his affect was alarming.

She straightened up, only to be enfolded in a tight embrace.

"Pixley!" Her cries were muffled by his plaid jacket.

"I've missed you, Fina."

He turned to Sergio. "I apologise for not meeting you on the other side, sir."

Sergio's eyebrows rose. "You're acquainted?"

Pixley adjusted his green tweed waistcoat. "Yes, I've had the pleasure of working with Miss Aubrey-Havelock on several assignments."

Bewildered, Fina opened her mouth and closed it.

"Well, that's fine, Marsh. Let's drive to the villa so I can get out of these wet clothes."

"Right away. I have a car waiting for us."

Fina and Pixley leaned their heads together as they followed Sergio's loping gait off the ferry.

"Marsh? Your new name?" hissed Fina.

Pixley nodded. "I'm his secretary."

"I gathered that, Sherlock."

Before she stepped into the car, Fina scanned Bellagio's dark blue lakefront and beautiful cream-coloured buildings. It was bitterly cold, and gazing at the snow-capped mountains only made her shiver more. She'd ask Pixley about skiing later.

Sergio slipped into the front seat, immediately engaging the elderly driver in lively Italian conversation.

As they were about to drive off, Fina's door opened.

"What the devil?" she cried.

"Oh, *scusi, Signorina.* We will travel with you to Villa Potenza. You are English, yes?"

The man bending into the car had a white bow tie, thinning blond-white, slicked-back hair, blindingly white teeth, and hands the size of focaccia loaves.

"Yes, I'm English. We can fit you in." Fina pinned Pixley to the other side of the car as she slid over.

"Not so close!" he protested.

"There's also a woman, you ninny," hissed Fina.

A lithe, petite woman with pencil-thin eyebrows, loose, wavy, dark brown hair, and a marvellous scarlet winter overcoat slid in next to Fina.

The man squeezed in after her.

The woman moved her shoulders to the side, along with her hips, so that, impossibly, she became half of her already petite size.

Fina and Pixley stared in wonder.

She giggled. "I'm Isa Fiore. Il Grande's assistant. And *sì*, I am a contortionist."

The man leaned over behind Isa. "I'm Il Grande Vittorio, the great magician. You've heard of me, yes?"

Blessedly, Sergio intervened from the front seat.

"Ah, the famous Il Grande. You're different from other magicians, aren't you?"

Vittorio puffed up his chest. "I am the best. I am stupendous. I am..."

"Modest," whispered Pixley.

"Pardon?"

"Oh, I was saying how *modish* you are. Fashionable."

Vittorio smoothed his blond-white moustache and grinned again, revealing sharp white teeth.

Fina twisted her head and peered out of the window as they came to a halt. The Villa Potenza's yellow exterior glowed in the morning light. Sergio turned from the front seat. "Don't let the simple exterior fool you. It's exquisite inside."

Pixley opened the door, holding onto the handle. Despite his efforts, the weight of the passengers behind him propelled him forward, onto the ground.

"Pix! Here, let me help you up."

Pixley held up a hand and lifted himself to his feet, dusting off his splendid tweed as he did so. "All part of how this day has already gone to hell."

Sergio dashed up the steps, shivering. Vittorio and Isa followed behind, each in a cape, one black and one purple. The driver unloaded the luggage.

Fina and Pixley admired the view overlooking Bellagio and the lake.

"Will you tell me why you're called Marsh and what is going on?" asked Fina.

"Remember I said I was sent on assignment to cover secret negotiations?"

"Yes, about the Abyssinian crisis. Italy's attack on Ethiopia. But how is the crisis connected to your secret name?"

"Well, I had to come undercover. They'd never let a journalist into secret negotiations."

"But you said you had been 'on assignment' with me to Sergio, which translates into journalist."

Pixley pushed his spectacles up his nose and sighed. "It's complicated."

"It would be."

"Would you be quiet and listen for a moment?"

Pixley rarely became irritated with her or anyone else, so Fina nodded.

"Sergio Chapman is a law professor at Cambridge—"

"I know—" Fina stopped herself.

Pixley grinned. "He is involved with these negotiations, though I'm not sure how. My editor told me Chapman would be in on the secret, but would treat me as a secretary. The slightly fake name is not to fool him, but to keep my identity secret from others."

Fina blinked. As Pixley was an Englishman with family roots in Ghana, white people often stared at him when they were travelling.

Pixley glowered. "I sense what you're thinking. I'm not stupid, remember?"

"No, no. I'm certain you have a plan."

He sighed. "Sorry, I'm on edge. I'll try to explain. For those who aren't aware of the negotiations, I'm a regular secretary. For those who are, Sergio will tell them I'm a specialist on Ethiopia."

"What kind of specialist?"

"An expert."

"But if there are other experts here, won't they find you out?"

Pixley puffed up his chest like Il Grande Vittorio. "I *am* an expert – as close to an expert as any journalist can be – on Italy's invasion. I'll be fine."

Another car drew up, disgorging the man who had rescued Sergio from drowning, along with a small, balding man with large black-framed spectacles, and a sprightly step. The bald man gathered up three briefcases, but dropped one, sending it flying in Fina and Pixley's direction.

The briefcase popped open, releasing a flutter of white papers.

"*Mein Gott!*" The man put his hands to his head and ran around in circles. The man in the brown suit had already disappeared into the villa, unaware of the scene below.

Fina and Pixley chased the papers, stomping on the escapees, with Pixley making little "aiieee" noises when he had success.

Fina scooped up a now-empty folder reading 'Sudan' across the top. She casually set it on top of the stack of papers and nodded. Pixley nodded back.

"*Seine papieren,*" said Pixley.

The bald man stared at him. Then he smiled, and said "*Danke. Vielen Dank.*" He looked from Fina to Pixley and back again.

"We're English," said Fina. "*Sprechen Sie Englisch?*"

"*Ach, ja.* Yes," he said.

"Splendid spectacles. Where did you purchase them?" asked Pixley.

The man removed his spectacles and peered at them. "Geneva. That's where I live."

Pixley stuck out his hand. "Pixley Marsh, secretary to Professor Chapman. This is Fina Aubrey-Havelock, assistant to Ruby Dove."

His eyes widened. "Ruby Dove? The one who makes frocks? But she is stupendous!"

Fina's mouth hung open. "You've met Ruby Dove?"

"*Nein*, but my wife, she follows fashion. Me, not so much. Every day she says she wants to buy a Ruby Dove frock! And I tell her, Jutta, *bitte*, Miss Dove is in London. She cannot make you a frock in Geneva." He gave them a happy shrug. "But it is a dream of hers." He paused. "I am forgetting myself. I'm Emil Pleischner. Secretary to Lord Mayhew, the man who was with me."

Pixley scratched his chin. "Lord Mayhew. Isn't he in Parliament? I remember he used to be an investor in – what was it?"

Emil squared the papers into a neat pile. "Yes. He is in the English Parliament. And he invested in armaments. But he is also on a special European commission, so I am his commission secretary."

With her best high-pitched, innocent voice, Fina said, "Is there going to be a commission meeting here?"

Emil's animated, elfin face froze. "No. Where did you get such an idea?"

A high, shrill scream saved Fina from answering.

3

The villa's carved wooden front door stood ajar. Emil pushed it wide open with one hand, while he clutched papers in the other.

"I'll kill her!" screamed a petite Jean Harlow-platinum-blonde woman, hands balled near her face. She wore a stunning fitted Schiaparelli gown and white mule sandals with white feathers. As she strutted toward the hall table, she flung a vase of dried flowers on the floor.

Pixley, Emil, and Fina jumped back. Glass shards spread across the stone floor like wildfire.

"Ach!" cried Emil. His spectacles tumbled off his nose as he clutched his face.

A butler glided up to Emil, grabbed his hand and led him away, while Pixley and Fina remained frozen.

The blonde woman's mouth stood open in horror, as if someone else were responsible for the disaster. Then she shook her head violently, though not a hair escaped from the grip of her upswept hairstyle. She glided toward them, around the lake of glass shards, with both hands outstretched. "Well, hello. You must be new staff?" she said, with a hint of malice and the faint twang of an American accent. Fina studied her face. She had fashionably thin eyebrows, large, doe-like brown eyes, a small mouth, high cheekbones, and a slight double chin, in contrast with her slim yet curvy figure. She jutted her chin upward in what Fina suspected was a self-conscious gesture, instead of innate haughtiness.

Pixley bowed. "At your service, Your Highness. I'm Pixley Marsh, secretary to Sergio Chapman. We met last night, but I realise you were immersed in preparations."

"Oh, poor Sergio. He stomped in here like a drowned rat." The marchesa's American accent subsided as she adopted the fluting tones of what she must have thought was an upper class English accent. "And who is this—" she paused, eying Fina with a slight grimace "—*lady*?"

Fina gulped. "I'm Fina Aubrey-Havelock. Assistant to Ruby Dove."

The marchesa brightened, though Fina wasn't sure if it was due to her double-barrelled name, or that of Ruby Dove. "Ah, but why are you working, sweetie, if you're an aristocrat?"

Pixley gave Fina a wicked grin.

"Not all of us have money. I'm not really an aristocrat."

"Pity..." The marchesa drifted away with her words, hand outstretched as if she were in a Shakespeare play.

Pixley cleared his throat. "May we be of assistance, Your Highness? As to whatever upset you?"

She turned her torso. "So kind. Planning a masked ball puts one under enormous strain. And I've just had some perfectly dreadful news. Marilyn Asher – you know, the American woman in British Parliament, who's a dear, dear friend – invited this, this, *woman*." She held her hands up to the ceiling in exasperation.

"Which woman?" asked Fina.

"Iveta Da Silva."

Fina glanced at Pixley. They had met Iveta on their Lisbon

adventure. She'd planned to return to Brazil with her daughter, Makeda, but apparently had been persuaded otherwise by this invitation.

"And she is a minx," continued the marchesa. "A strumpet. A hussy. A—"

The door creaked open behind them.

In walked a thin woman in a forest-green suit, white beret, and white gloves. Her clothes were not expensive, but they were exquisitely cut to create a tailored yet slightly oversized appearance. Her posture was impeccable, but Fina sensed it was tension that held her thin frame upright, rather than finishing-school training. Her Oxford heels were silent – impossibly so – as she crossed the threshold. She set down her suitcase, slid her large white clutch under her arm, and held out a hand to Pixley. She smiled at Fina and the marchesa.

Pixley's eyes widened. "But, but, you're Hazel Padmore! Here!" He continued to shake her hand, unable to stop. "I say, haven't we met before? Were you at one of the meetings for Ethiopia?" He snapped his fingers. "You spoke at it!"

Though Hazel remained stiff, a smile relaxed her face. "Yes, I'm vice-chair of the International African Friends of Abyssinia. Though I was just introducing our main speaker. I'm not disposed to be on stage."

"My, my, plenty of famous people in that outfit. How thrilling." Then he cleared his throat, his voice going an octave lower. "And important."

"I'm also the secretary to the empress. The temporarily deposed Empress of Ethiopia."

The marchesa sniffed, clearly put out at being upstaged by a guest. Then she grinned as she once again navigated around the glass.

"So glad you joined us, Miss Padmore. King Selassie spoke of you incessantly when I met him in London. He said you'd be able to write my memoirs in a few weeks."

Hazel cocked her head to one side. "Too kind, Marchesa Della Corsini—"

"Please call me Marchesa Gloria—"

"Though I believe he meant I could gather enough material to write your memoirs in a few weeks, not complete them. It will take considerably longer. I plan to write them when I visit my family in Ethiopia."

"But my dear! You must stay here to write them – it is too dangerous to travel to Ethiopia."

Hazel pursed her lips.

Pixley intervened. "You must be exhausted after your journey."

The tall, thin butler reappeared behind them, his hooded eyes remaining at half-mast. He stared at the broken glass and snapped his fingers.

"Your Highness, Miss Padmore and Miss Aubrey-Havelock have had long journeys. Would you mind awfully if we meet with you later?" Pixley asked.

Ignoring his comment, the marchesa barked, "Gustavo. Have Daria clean up this mess while you show Miss Padmore and Miss—"

"Aubrey-Havelock," supplied Fina.

"Y-e-s," the marchesa said doubtfully. "Show them to their rooms."

Gustavo led them through the black-and-white marble foyer, up to a palatial marble staircase, fitted with red rugs and gold cherub statues on either side.

"Crikey," whispered Fina to Pixley, as she glanced up at the carved ceilings with gold leaves and frescos of biblical stories.

Hazel followed behind them. Fina had never known anyone

make so little noise, though she noticed Hazel checked her watch at least ten times on their way up the stairs.

Gustavo removed a grapefruit-sized keyring from his pocket and unlocked the first door to the right. The corner of his small, insolent mouth twitched as he jiggled the key.

"Please." He motioned Fina to the door.

She twisted the handle. Nothing happened.

Gustavo grinned. "Ah, just a little joke."

Fina looked at Hazel and Pixley for confirmation that Gustavo was a most inappropriate butler.

He opened the door, but did not offer an apology.

"Mmm..." said Pixley. "Your room is the Poodle Suite."

"What do you mean, 'poodle'?" asked Fina.

Pixley pointed at the door nameplate. "It's the marchesa's little joke, I suppose. At least, I hope it's a joke. All of the rooms are named after dog breeds. Mine's the Greyhound."

"I take it she loves dogs."

"She does, but the house is filled with cats."

Gustavo cleared his throat. "Her Highness is most fond of dogs, but is still heartbroken since she left hers in New York."

As if on cue, a tabby cat wrapped its tail around Pixley's legs. "Shoo, shoo...you blasted beast. You'll get fur all over my trousers!"

The tabby glared at Pixley and padded toward Fina, who was already crouching down. "Come here, sweetums," she cooed. Hazel and Pixley glanced at each other and shook their heads.

"Come here, Puffy." Fina waved the cat into the room. The tabby halted at the doorway. Fina scanned the room, shoulders slumping.

Pixley popped his head over her shoulder. "Let's rename this the Ebenezer Scrooge Suite. Why is Marchesa Gloria cross with you?"

The room – though cupboard would be a better description

– was a long, narrow rectangle, with one tiny window. The truncated bed appeared to be from the Middle Ages, when people were shorter and slept sitting up. A basin with a water jug stood in one corner, near a small chest of drawers. At least it was clean, she thought, trying to find an upside to the room.

"Where's the lavatory and bath?" asked Fina.

"Down the hallway, miss," said Gustavo.

"Come with me, Feens," said Pixley. "Leave your suitcase here and join me in the lap of luxury."

Leaving Gustavo to take Hazel to her room, Fina followed Pixley.

As they strolled down the corridor, a door opened and a flurry of purple-and-red velvet flapped against her head.

4

"Ow!" cried Fina, more out of fear than pain. The purple-and-red flashes reminded her of their nemesis – nicknamed Moriarty – who had been following them for months. Fina's heart slowed as she spied a small woman in her late thirties – shorter than herself – fidgeting with scissors and thread. Her dangling diamond earrings brushed against her high gold collar. On anyone else, it would have looked gauche. On her, it looked clean and minimal.

The woman's dark brown head snapped upward. Her high chignon stayed in place, despite the sudden motion. "I am Zora. Who are you?"

Pixley pushed past Fina and grasped Zora's tiny hand. "Madam Zora. What a pleasure it is to meet you. I've followed all of your adventures, and I—"

Madam Zora's eyes flashed and then crinkled up warmly. "How kind, how kind. And you are?"

"Pixley Marsh. Special attaché to Professor Chapman."

"How glamorous. I've never met a special attaché before."

Fina smiled. Now Pixley was a special attaché, not just a secretary.

"And who is this charming young woman?" Zora surveyed Fina with a critical eye.

Fina crumpled inwardly from the frank scrutiny. "I'm Fina Aubrey-Havelock. Assistant to Ruby Dove."

"Ah, the famous Ruby Dove. Where is she? I am looking forward to meeting her." Zora tapped her foot. She had the frenetic energy of a terrier. Fina glanced at her door's nameplate. It read 'Basset Hound'.

"She'll arrive this afternoon." Fina paused. "I am such an admirer of your work, Zora. The Paris season's emerald gown was divine."

"And I hope you'll continue to design men's clothes," put in Pixley. "I've been saving up to purchase your fabulous red jumper."

Zora turned to Pixley. "I may have something for you," she said with a twinkle in her eye. "We must discuss later. Over a glass of... what do you English prefer? Oh yes, sherry."

Without another word, she spun on her heel and shut the door.

Pixley pulled down his green waistcoat. "Well. Madam Zora. Here. Did you know she was a guest?"

"Not a clue. But she likes you, Pix! We'd better prepare you for your date with destiny."

They entered Pixley's room, which was a considerable step up from Fina's blasted poodle cupboard. Though small in size, the room exuded warmth and comfort. Mellow burgundy walls met thick, plush rugs scattered across the marble floor. A large four-poster bed dominated the room, next to a gleaming roll-top desk and a balcony.

"I'll trade you," giggled Fina.

"Not on your life." Pixley peered over his spectacles at her. "But you're welcome to spend daytime in here." He opened the French windows. "Behold the splendour."

A frozen pond stood next to a glassed-over winter garden with orange trees. A woman with a daring hat and mink wrapped lazily around her neck flicked cigarette ash into the pond. Fina guessed she was in her fifties. Next to her stood Lord Mayhew, running his finger around the inside of his hat.

Fina waved at Pixley to crouch down. He looked at her quizzically, shrugged, and bent over. Though he soon gave up his crouch and sat on the balcony floor.

"Is everything ready?" asked the woman.

"Yes, and there's plenty of cash waiting for us on the other side," replied Mayhew.

"*Signore, scusi.*" A voice rose behind them.

Fina jumped and her hand fluttered on her chest. She spotted a maid's uniform, obscured by a stack of towels.

"What are you being?" the maid asked.

"Yes, Daria, what can we do for you?" asked Pixley, rising from the floor as if it were a perfectly natural place to sit on a cold winter's day.

A head wrapped in a scarf popped out from behind the towels. "More towels."

Pixley motioned to the dressing table.

Fina surveyed Daria. Blonde hair peeked out from behind her scarf, though it appeared to be her natural colour, unlike the marchesa's hair. Though she was light-boned, she towered over Pixley and Fina, even in her serviceable flat shoes. Her well-groomed face was blank.

Pixley strode indoors. "Tell me, Daria. Who else is expected this afternoon?"

She twisted her index finger at the corner of her mouth. "Lady Asher arrived. Miss Da Silva and Miss Dove will also come soon."

"When is the masked ball?" asked Fina.

"Tomorrow night. You have your costumes, yes?" she asked.

"Not yet. Though I cannot fathom how I'll find one by tomorrow night."

"In the cellar. There are trunks of costumes. You may find one there."

Daria marched out.

Fina's stomach rumbled.

Pixley glanced at his watch. "It's 11:30 and lunch isn't until noon. I need to read through a few documents before our first meeting after lunch."

"You mean the secret negotiations?"

Pixley tapped the side of his nose and grinned.

"Oh, don't be so insufferably gauche."

He sighed. "I can tell you're hungry because you're insulting me. Why don't you unpack and we'll meet up downstairs in the dining room?"

"Sorry," she whispered. "Everything irritates me when I'm hungry."

"Don't worry," said Pixley. "I've learned not to take it personally."

Fina's face turned hot as she slumped away. Pixley was irritated with her, the marchesa thought she was worthless, and she had no role to play, other than a lowly assistant to the great Ruby Dove. At least the large tabby was there to greet her when she reached her room. The cat meowed plaintively and held up one paw, like a dog begging for food.

"Hmm..." said Fina to the cat. "A man on the train gave me a sardines tin which he said would make me more intelligent." She rummaged through her suitcase and held the tin aloft. The cat mewed louder. Fina turned the tin's key and set it in the corridor, then shut the door so the odour wouldn't ruin her clothes. As usual, her meagre, though beloved, wardrobe took two minutes to unpack.

A knock came at the door.

As Fina rose, a slip of paper slid out from underneath her luggage. It read 'save me' in Italian. What an odd place to put a note – someone must have entered her room, because the note definitely hadn't been there before. That person must be desperate, especially desperate if they put the note in her room and not Ruby's! Why would anyone trust her? People did say she had a kind face.

The knocking resumed.

Fina stuffed the note into her pocket and opened the door.

Lord Mayhew. He frowned and flared his nostrils. Fina peered at the smooth, chiselled, flat facial lines, and wide, sensuous mouth. And enormous ears. The only wrinkles on his fiftyish face were under his eyes, set permanently at half-mast, looking like little pond ripples.

She laughed inwardly as she realised Lord Mayhew should have been in Madam Zora's room. Though he was handsome, his resemblance to a basset hound was alarming.

"Yes?"

"Clean up this mess. It positively reeks to high heaven." He held out a few coins. "There's a good girl."

"Oh, but I'm not a maid," said Fina.

But Mayhew had vanished.

Fina rushed back down the corridor and tapped on Pixley's door. "It's Fina."

"I'm dressing, what is it?"

"I need to talk to you. Now."

The door flung open. Pixley wore a blindingly red jumper. He smiled. "Spiffing, isn't it? I hope it will remind Madam Zora about her jumper."

"I have more important things to discuss than jumpers," grumbled Fina as she pushed past him.

"Hey! Sourpusses aren't allowed. We're on holiday."

Fina pulled out two crumpled sheets of paper and handed them to Pixley.

He unfolded the first one. "*Save me.* Where did you find it?"

"Someone must have put it on my bed after I set down my suitcase. I'm sure it wasn't there when I came in."

"The handwriting is scrawled, so maybe it's someone who isn't used to writing."

"The next note is more important." She handed him the flybill from the ferry dock.

He let out a low whistle. "*Criminale.*"

Fina tapped her foot. "Well?"

Pixley peered at her over his reading glasses. "It's dangerous to discuss when you're hungry, but I can tell we won't have lunch unless I explain."

"You've got that right, mister," said Fina in a parody of the marchesa's accent.

Pixley plopped down on the bed. "It's simple, really. I have a brother."

5

"You have a brother?" screeched Fina.

"Shh! People will hear you. The walls are thin." He sighed. "We're not twins, but we do resemble each other. I'm younger by two years."

"What's his name?"

"Ernest. Rather ironic."

"Why?"

Pixley rubbed his forehead. "He's anything but earnest. He's a devious snake in the grass."

Fina paced around a small rug, unconsciously mimicking Ruby's favourite pastime. "Pix! I've never heard you be so unkind about someone close to you."

Pixley whipped out a matchbox and set the crumpled paper alight. He tossed the glowing ball into an empty jug.

Fina stopped and crossed her arms. "What good will it do? And why do the Italians believe him to be a criminal?"

"Because he is a criminal. And I don't mean he breaks the law for a good cause. He's greedy and impulsive. Always has been. Even when we were kids, he'd swipe food off my plate, even though he hadn't finished his own."

"Pixley Hayford! I could never imagine a relative of yours being so selfish." She paused. "Is he in Italy? Has he been in contact?"

"No, I haven't heard from him in years." He sighed, slapped his thighs and stood up. "Let's go to lunch."

Fina stared at him. "But don't you understand? If I saw this drawing at the ferry dock, there must be others in Bellagio. People will mistake him for you."

Pixley shrugged. "What can I do? Not leave the villa? Besides, I have a passport. I'd explain to the authorities he's my brother."

"Why would they believe you?"

Pixley snapped open his briefcase and pulled out a folder brimming with newspaper clippings. "These are my alibis. They prove that I couldn't have been in certain places at certain times. If I know my brother – and I surely do – he will have been on a thieving spree. I'm certain I can line up the dates if I must."

The lunch gong sounded below.

FINA SLURPED HER CONSOMMÉ, moving the spoon slowly and steadily to avoid spatter on her blue dress. Pixley stuck a napkin in over his collar and ate with delicate abandon, as only Pixley could.

Finally giving up on her soup, Fina surveyed the view from the glassed-in terrace overlooking Bellagio. Maybe she and Pixley ought to explore the winding, narrow streets this afternoon while Ruby rested from her journey. She wondered if the jolly ferry steaming toward them carried Miss Ruby Dove aboard.

"Feens. Are you there?"

"Oh, yes. Sorry. Where are Lady Asher and Iveta?

The marchesa, Madam Zora, Sergio, and Lord Mayhew sat at one table, while Hazel, Vittorio, and Isa were at another. Lord Mayhew and the marchesa were close. Very close. Madam Zora and Sergio made laughing conversation.

"Dar-lings! But how divine! You're in Italy!"

Iveta Da Silva, resplendent in a turquoise caftan-style dress, glided into the dining room. She flung her arms out, nearly blinding Fina with the reflecting sparkle of her many gemstone rings. A large emerald pendant threatened to disappear into her ample bosom. Fina reflected that she had never seen the jewellery dealer wear the same stones twice.

At top speed, she made her way to Fina and Pixley's table. Fina and Pixley stood up in tandem, ready for Iveta's bear-like embrace. She kissed their cheeks, hugged them and surveyed each one as if they were children who had grown.

The silence around them was deafening.

Out of the corner of her eye, Fina noticed the marchesa scowl and snap her napkin.

"*Carinho!* But what are you doing here? How delightful!" Iveta frowned. "Where is Ruby? I must see my Ruby!" She waved her arms once again in a dramatic gesture, sending her sleeves billowing over Pixley's bald pate.

Painfully self-conscious they were part of a 'scene', Fina pressed down lightly on one of Iveta's arms. "Please join us for lunch. We'll tell you everything."

Iveta smiled and nodded, heaving her statuesque figure into the small rattan chair. As Pixley was recounting their adventures to Iveta, another woman walked in.

Unlike Iveta, who glided like an apparition – a substantive apparition – this woman marched. She was the one who had spoken to Lord Mayhew, outside Pixley's window. Her tight burgundy-rouged mouth and rigid posture were offset by a soft, elegant navy dress with perforated bishop sleeves and a long strand of pearls. As she glanced at the tables, her eyelids flick-ered. There was only one vacant seat – at Fina's table.

She clutched her bag and weaved through the ocean of white linen.

Pursing her lips, she scraped back a chair and set her bag across the back of it. She held out a gloved hand. "Lady Marilyn Asher."

So this was the woman MP. She certainly cut an authorita-tive figure. "Fina Aubrey-Havelock. This is Iveta Da Silva and Pixley, er, Marsh."

Lady Asher's eyes slewed toward Iveta and Pixley. After a long pause, she gave her hand to Pixley and then nodded at Iveta.

Iveta's eyes flashed with playful malice. "But darling, those pearls! Where did you purchase them?"

"They were given to me by Lord Bavenstoke-Barnard."

"Was this lord a joking kind?"

Lady Asher held her fork midway to her mouth. "Nothing of the sort. A perfect gentleman."

"You must not be carried away by these aristocrats, darling. As an American, you are easy prey. They have many tricks up their jackets," said Iveta.

"Tricks!" Vittorio turned toward them. "Shall I perform a few tricks?"

Iveta turned around in her seat. "Perhaps you will transform these fake pearls into real pearls, Il Grande Vittorio?"

Lady Asher dabbed the corners of her mouth and threw down her napkin.

She marched out, her perfectly coiffed, upswept hairstyle threatening to topple over.

"Well," whispered Pixley. "I cannot say I'm sad she toddled off. Now I can enjoy my lunch."

Iveta put her hand over Pixley's. "The woman is dreadful.

She is all tight inside. I can tell she does not enjoy life very much."

Fina smiled at Iveta. Here was a woman who truly enjoyed life, even if it put her in tight spots. "I'm perplexed. The marchesa said Lady Asher invited you to the villa. Is it true?"

Iveta wagged a graceful finger at Fina. "Ah, I forgot. The detectives." She shrugged. "It is true, Lady Asher invited me. I have connections with the Brazilian embassy. She wishes to retire in Brazil and it might benefit her. The warm weather might loosen her tight limbs."

"But how could you help her retire in Brazil?" asked Pixley.

"I am bored. Let us discuss something amusing, darlings," she said. "Such as – darling Ruby!"

They all looked up.

Ruby Dove stood in the doorway, clad in her favourite grey travelling suit.

She grimaced and then tumbled to the floor.

6

"Ruby!" screamed Fina, Iveta, and Pixley in unison. They flung back their chairs and rushed to her side.

Fina lifted Ruby's head while Pixley took her pulse. Iveta stood over them, fluttering her arms.

"Her pulse is steady," sighed Pixley. "She must have fainted."

The villa's guests gathered in a tight circle.

Iveta shooed them away. "Please, she must have air."

Pixley nodded at Iveta and they lifted Ruby. Fina kept her friend's head steady.

"Gustavo!" called Marchesa Gloria. "Help them carry Miss Dove to the Labrador Retriever Suite."

Out of breath, Gustavo led them up the stairs. As Fina walked backwards, she glimpsed the crowd below. All appeared worried, save Vittorio. The corner of his mouth was upturned in a sinister grin. Maybe it was part of his magician's act.

As Iveta and Pixley laid Ruby down on the enormous bed in the sumptuous suite, Fina removed her navy Renzo Carnevali shoes.

Gustavo peered at Ruby's face. "May I?" he asked. "I have some doctor's training."

The trio nodded at one another.

Gustavo pulled up one eyelid and opened her mouth. He then scribbled in a small notebook, tore out a sheet and handed it to Pixley.

"Cordyceps militaris," Pixley read slowly.

"What is it?" asked Fina.

Gustavo scratched his head. "Those things that grow in the darkness. Fungi."

"Mushrooms?" asked Iveta.

"*Sì*, mushrooms, *signora. Grazie.*"

"Where do we find them?" asked Fina, suspiciously. She did not trust mushrooms, though she'd always enjoyed foraging adventures as a girl.

Gustavo scribbled again and handed the paper to Pixley. "*Farmacia*. In town. I will give you directions. Our staff would go but we are most busy in preparations."

Iveta had already nestled into a green velvet chair next to Ruby. "I will watch over dear Ruby while you go to the pharmacy."

Pixley and Fina looked at each other. Iveta was sweet on Ruby, so it seemed safe to leave her in Iveta's care.

"We'll go." Pixley glanced at his watch. "But I must return by two o'clock for the meeting."

"I'll fetch my overcoat and handbag." Fina left Ruby's room and padded down the corridor. Her door was ajar. Using her forefinger, she tapped it lightly. It squeaked open, revealing – nothing. The door lock looked normal. Shrugging, she scooped up her overcoat and handbag, but not before noticing her handbag was open.

Drat.

She gave a sigh of relief as she riffled through her wallet. Everything was in order. Then her heart leapt into her throat.

She leaned into the corridor and called, "Pixley! Would you come here?"

Pixley locked the door to his room and trundled toward her. "What is it?"

"Someone stole my passport."

"Have you emptied your bag?"

With shaking hands, she emptied her bag onto the dusty bed. "Nothing. But they didn't steal money, so it's unlikely to be a desperate member of the staff."

Pixley removed a handkerchief from his breast pocket and wiped his forehead. "I'm certain we can arrange it with the consulate."

"There's a consulate in Bellagio?"

"That's one reason the negotiations are being held here."

Fina sighed. "A thorny problem, but I suppose you're right. It's the weekend, so I'll try there on Monday."

"Let's go to the pharmacy before anything else happens, shall we?"

A SHARP GUST of wind hit Fina's face, and then soft sunlight warmed it as they walked down the steep cobblestone hill into town. Even in the dead of winter, the town's warm colours could not be dulled. They wound their way around a pink house with green shutters ,next to a trattoria featuring a surly cook out front. He nodded at them as he blew smoke rings into the blue sky.

Fina nearly tripped over a sleeping cat as she turned the corner. She glanced up and spied Hazel Padmore and Emil Pleischner walking toward a small square. Hazel glided while Emil loped beside her with his hands behind his back.

She grabbed Pixley and pulled him into a doorway just as Hazel turned her head.

"What are you doing?" hissed Pixley.

"Didn't you see Emil and Hazel?"

"So?"

"Were they acquainted before? Why would the secretary to the empress and Lord Mayhew's assistant be friends? And what are they doing in town?"

"What's so odd? They're both guests. Perhaps they both wanted to stroll into town."

Fina shook her head. "I have a feeling."

"Here we go with your feelings."

She glared at him. Pixley smiled sheepishly. "You're right, you're right. Those feelings have been right before."

The door they were leaning against suddenly opened, sending them tumbling inside.

A woman in an apron and headscarf loomed over them, hands on hips.

"What are you doing? Get out of my house!" she cried in Italian.

"Gladly," said Pixley, as Fina offered a hand up. They bowed, nodded, said "*scusi*" three times, and scurried into the street.

"Look!" Fina pointed to a stone church. "They've gone inside. Let's follow." She pulled out a blue silk scarf and wrapped it around her head as they slipped inside.

A crumpled, gnome-like woman with thick spectacles on a chain nodded at them as they tiptoed across the stone paving.

Hazel and Emil stood at the altar, lighting candles.

Emil had a bandage under one eye, which must have been due to his injury from the shattered vase. His hand shook as he lit a candle. Hazel's hand was perfectly steady.

Fina and Pixley ran to a column on either side of the nave.

The gnome woman peered at them suspiciously.

Fina smiled and nodded her head, though she had no idea why her smiles would mollify the woman. Peeking around the corner, she watched Hazel and Emil slide into a pew. Nearby, a mop leaned against a column. Maybe the cleaner was on a smoke break. Fina pulled her kerchief farther over her forehead, covering her profile. Then she grabbed the mop and swiped it furiously down the aisle near Emil and Hazel.

She looked up and saw Pixley engaging the gnome woman in quiet conversation, using his bulk to block her from seeing Fina.

"But we must stop him," whispered Hazel.

"How? He is formidable. With these hordes of people around, it will be difficult," replied Emil.

Fina held her breath, listening intently.

She moved closer.

Someone tapped her shoulder.

7

Ruby's gritty eyes peeled open. She jerked up, blinking in the darkness.

She heard a door click.

Weak and sweaty, she collapsed back into bed and stared upward.

A movement prompted her eyes to slew downward, over to the door. A figure sat hunched over, snoring gently. Ruby's eyes couldn't focus – at least not in the darkness, so she switched on the bedside lamp.

The figure's head flopped upright. Iveta. "*Meu amor*, you're awake! But how marvellous."

Ruby blinked. "Iveta? What are you doing here?"

"Someone invited me, *carinho*." She waved her hands dismissively as she glided to a chair next to Ruby. "That does not matter. What matters is whether you are feeling better now."

"What happened? I remember seeing a dining room, but then everything blacked out."

Iveta placed a cold compress on her forehead. "You fainted, poor thing, though you did not revive, so we brought you here. Did you have a trying journey?"

"It was rather trying – both trains were late, and we had to stand shivering outside. I suspect the real reason, however, was what happened when I went to the San Pellegrino thermal baths. Because my connecting train was late, we had oodles of time, and San Pellegrino was nearby."

"I'll plan to visit San Pellegrino. Was the water as delightful as everyone says?"

"Spiffing. Though I didn't follow their instructions to drink water and eat lightly."

"Well, you must have water now, and then you will – how do the English say? You'll be right as the ocean."

Ruby didn't want to correct her, so she took a sip. Much better.

Iveta picked up a tissue-covered packet from the bedside table. "This must be the prescription from your friends."

Ruby sighed, relieved Fina and Pixley hadn't abandoned her. "I wondered where they were. How long have I been unconscious?"

Iveta glanced at a wall clock. "Perhaps an hour." She emptied the packet into the water glass and stirred, making a gentle clanging noise. "Here, drink this."

Ruby stared at the brown concoction. She hesitated.

Iveta touched Ruby's chin. "Do you want to feel better for the party?"

Ruby nodded and took the glass.

She held it to her lips.

FINA SPUN ROUND. It was the same woman whose house they'd invaded. This time, instead of an open mouth, her lips were pursed and her shoulders stiff. She grabbed Fina's mop.

Before Fina could receive the scolding of a lifetime, she dashed to the door. Pixley nodded at the gnome woman and followed Fina. They fled across the square, scattering startled pigeons. A child screeched. A circle of old men grumbled as they flew past them.

Once around the corner, they halted, leaning over and heaving.

Pixley wiped his bald head with a handkerchief. Then he chuckled. Soon the chuckles became a belly laugh. "Jupiter's teeth, Feens! You do cut it fine."

Fina looked up. Shopkeepers stared at them from behind windows and open doors. She approached a tall, cadaverous man and said, *"Farmacia?"*

The man grunted and pointed down the street. Fina grabbed Pixley's arm and pulled him away. "Let's not draw more attention to ourselves, shall we?"

"You started it, dearest." Pixley glanced at his watch. "We'd better look lively. I'll be late to the meeting and Sergio won't forgive me."

Around the next corner, she spotted a large enamel sign reading 'farmacista' atop a small doorway.

A merry bell clanged as they entered a well-lit shop, stocked from top to bottom with colourful bottles and tins. The afternoon sun filtered through a window, creating a kaleidoscope of colours and flashes of silver from the tins. Distracted by the shiny objects, Fina inspected a display with an image of a happy woman skipping down a garden path.

"We're here for Ruby, remember?" hissed Pixley through a corner of his mouth.

"Sorry. Do you have the prescription?"

Pixley handed her the crumpled note.

A small man peered over reading spectacles and frowned. *"Come posso aiutarla?"*

Fina understood Italian, but speaking it was another matter. She slid the paper across the counter.

The man's bushy eyebrows disappeared into his thick thatch of hair. He held up a finger, turned, and disappeared into the shop's nether regions.

Fina drummed her fingers on the counter. "I'm not keen on these mushrooms."

"But it's a pharmacy. Surely they wouldn't dispense a harmful drug."

The merry shop bell clanged.

Lord Mayhew strode in. He slowed, his face turning orchid-purple. "Miss Aubrey-Havelock, Mr Marsh." He nodded. "I have what you young people call a jiffy tummy after lunch. As I have a long afternoon ahead, I decided I'd better attend to it."

Odd, thought Fina. A Member of Parliament becoming so flustered over a pharmacy encounter.

"We're here to pick up remedies for Miss Dove." Pixley pushed his spectacles up his nose and peered at Lord Mayhew.

Lord Mayhew shrank back, but then stiffened, recovering his bearing. "Yes, I hope she recovers soon – must have been the strain of travel. Women—"

"I believe she's ill," interjected Fina. She hesitated. Ought she to ask him why he had thought she was a maid? She plunged forward. "I'm curious. Why did you assume I was one of the staff when you met me earlier? When you knocked on my door and asked me to clean up?"

He ran his finger around his stiff collar. "Quite natural, really. I saw the maid – what's her name?"

"Daria," supplied Pixley.

"Yes, I noticed Daria leave your room earlier. So I assumed it was Daria's room."

"But Daria could be in any room. She's a maid," said Pixley.

"Yes, but Miss Aubrey-Havelock's room was so tiny, I assumed it was a servant's."

Fina sighed. "You're right. It is impossibly small."

Mayhew grinned. "Marchesa Gloria must hold a grudge against you. Pity. She's a fascinating woman."

Fina balled her fist. "Why is it a pity?"

Pixley grabbed Fina's arm and said hurriedly, "It was nice chatting, Lord Mayhew, but we really must rush back to Miss Dove."

Lord Mayhew tipped his hat and turned to the pharmacist.

Pixley pushed Fina outside.

"WHY WERE YOU PUSHING ME? I was just warming up to our friend." asked Fina.

"Because I feared, dear Red, you were about to spark an altercation. I know you."

"But the man irritates me."

"Why? He seems a perfectly decent chap. Excellent clothes, though brown isn't his colour."

Fina snorted and walked up the cobblestone hill.

Pixley ran after her, panting. He finally caught up. "Did you eat something peculiar for lunch?"

Fina glared at him. "Oh yes, that's right. Sensitive Fina must not have had enough to eat. I've had enough of your food jokes today."

Pixley clenched his jaw and then dissolved into a fit of giggles.

A cat stared at them from the doorway.

"You're making a scene – the cat's staring at us. What's so funny?"

"You. When you're cross, you're such a different person."

He put a hand on her shoulder and looked at his watch. "I must fly."

Fina stared at the cat, watching it lap up dirty water in a bowl. She wouldn't let a cat drink water like that. Cat... water... Ruby. Fina turned and rushed up the hill.

"What's put a bee in your bonnet?" asked Pixley.

"Ruby. We must see Ruby. Now."

8

"Don't drink it, Ruby!" yelled Fina.

Pixley rushed into Ruby's room and grabbed the glass, causing droplets to fly everywhere. Fina glanced at the bedspread. The spots where the droplets had fallen were now little holes.

"Selkies and kelpies. It's acid!"

Ruby put her hands to her mouth and leapt out of bed.

Iveta screamed and ran into the corridor.

Quivering, Ruby bent over and inspected the bedspread. "Acid turned the bedspread blue here. That means a few possibilities..."

Pixley gradually lifted Ruby upright and moved her backwards into a chair. "Sit down, dear Ruby. You've had a shock."

"But the bedspread is blue."

"Yes, dear heart, but the acid type is immaterial. All that matters is it was acid. Someone was trying to kill you."

Fina sat down on a bench next to Ruby. She peered at her friend. Despite their many scrapes with danger, she'd never seen Ruby so shaken. Maybe she was already weak.

Gustavo and Daria appeared in the doorway. "Miss Da Silva screamed, but she wouldn't tell us what happened. Is Miss Dove injured?"

Pixley adjusted his spectacles. "No, she's had a lucky escape. If Fina hadn't had a premonition..."

Fina gulped. "Gustavo. Daria. Has anyone been in this room?"

They shrugged in unison. Daria's eyelid twitched.

Gustavo coughed. "After you two went to town, I fetched water and a few digestive biscuits for Miss Da Silva. She requested them. Then I closed the door and went about my duties."

"Did you shut the door?" asked Fina.

"I believe so," said Gustavo.

"I noticed the door was ajar when we arrived," said Fina. "Which might mean someone slipped in. Someone *must* have slipped in."

"Unless it was Miss Da Silva," said Daria. Then she held her hand over her mouth. Gustavo glared at her.

Pixley lit a cigarette. "Why do you suspect Miss Da Silva?"

"Oh, no, no, I should not have said such a thing. It just occurred to me she might have done it."

"Did you notice the open door, Daria, when you were cleaning the rooms?" asked Pixley.

"No, I did not. But I only walked by once."

"I suppose neither of you spotted anyone go into this room," said Pixley.

Gustavo and Daria shook their heads.

Voices from the corridor grew louder, and Madam Zora and Marchesa Gloria appeared in the doorway. Gustavo whispered to them, presumably telling them what had happened.

Iveta returned, fluttering past Marchesa Gloria and Madam

Zora. "My precious gem, will you forgive me? I must have fallen asleep and someone tried to poison you!" Ruby disappeared within Iveta's embrace.

"You did not hear anyone come in?" asked Fina.

"But no, *carinho*. But no! I ate a few biscuits and drank an espresso. I ought to have been alert, not asleep."

Pixley and Fina exchanged glances.

"Gustavo. You didn't tell us you served Miss Da Silva an espresso."

Gustavo's hooded eyes lowered. "Ah, but it is so commonplace I did not think about it."

Iveta scrunched up her face. "It was so bitter, darling. So bitter."

~

As the hubbub of the opening of negotiations hummed around him, Pixley stared at his trousers' knife-pleat. He frowned. It wasn't sharp enough.

"Mr Marsh. Would you find the Addis file?" Sergio Chapman stubbed out his cigarette.

"Certainly." Pixley's fingers worked rapidly, inching their way through the suitcase files. He pulled out a brown envelope and handed it to Sergio.

Lord Mayhew stood up and pressed his fingertips against the gleaming oval oak table. "Now, gentlemen – I mean, ladies and gentlemen," he said, nodding at Marilyn Asher and Hazel Padmore. "We may begin negotiations. We are gathered here today..."

Pixley had interviewed many politicians in his time. As a result, he had practice smiling and nodding at them while they droned on. He did that now, staring admiringly at Lord Mayhew, occasionally nodding, all while surreptitiously scanning the mirrored room. That's how the marchesa had introduced it, calling it 'the Mirror Room' a suitable name if ever there was one. Floor-to-ceiling mirrors hung arm's-width apart, lending a cheerful airiness to the heavy topic of the negotiations. Though it was an odd choice for a diplomatic discussion, given the tendency to stare at oneself – or others – in the mirror opposite.

Hazel Padmore had changed into an elegant wine-coloured suit, though she still wore her long string of pearls. Her impassive face indicated that she, too, was bored by Mayhew's speech. He wondered why she was at the negotiations. Hadn't she been invited here to write Marchesa Gloria's memoirs? And why wouldn't the marchesa have chosen a professional writer for the job?

As if in answer to his question, Pixley heard Mayhew say, "And thank you to Miss Padmore for stepping in with her excellent shorthand skills at the last minute."

Peculiar. Surely he or Emil Pleischner would have been the ones to take notes. He sighed. Even though they were secretaries, he supposed Mayhew expected a woman to take notes.

Sergio glanced again at Miss Padmore. For the fifth time. Hmmm... something brewing there.

Pixley turned his attention to Marilyn Asher, who was spending an inordinate amount of time staring into the button eyes of the poor mink wrapped around her shoulders.

Emil sat opposite Marilyn, next to Mayhew. He would occasionally look up from sorting papers to nod and offer his elfin smile to Mayhew, but was otherwise engrossed in his sorting tasks.

It was certainly an odd assortment of characters for such a high-powered negotiation. Scarcely the crowd you'd expect to decide Ethiopia's fate. Most of these people, Pixley mused, must not be who they seemed.

Mayhew sat down and shuffled papers. "Let us begin."

Pixley lit a cigarette, while Mayhew dispensed with further preliminaries. Spiffing villa, he thought as he turned his attention to the carved wood panels, plush rugs, and priceless vases scattered throughout the room. Behind Lord Mayhew sat a life-size painting of Napoleon – one of the few paintings in the room, given that the wall space belonged to the mirrors. Interesting choice for an Italian villa, but it must have been Marchesa Gloria's touch.

As he stared at Napoleon's pale, round face, he saw something flicker. Pixley removed his spectacles and rubbed his eyes. He replaced them and blinked – perhaps it was a trick of the light from the mirrors. What the devil? Napoleon's eyes had moved!

Fighting the urge to leap up, he whispered in Sergio's ear, "Must dash to the loo."

Sergio frowned but he nodded.

Pixley rose, put up a deprecating hand, and toddled past Sergio and behind Lord Mayhew. He peered up at Napoleon. The emperor looked perfectly normal. His eyes didn't move.

In the corridor, Pixley spied Daria marching toward the stairs. "Psst... Daria!" He waved her over.

"*Sì, signore?*"

"You know this villa well, don't you? Are there any secret passages?"

"Secret–?" She looked at him quizzically.

"Ah, holes, places to hide?"

"Signore wants to hide?" She gave him a coquettish smile.

"No, no, I don't want to hide, but I spotted someone behind the Napoleon painting in there." He pointed to the Mirror Room.

Daria shrugged. "I do not understand, but I have only

worked here a year. Perhaps Gustavo will know." She walked away with a tiny shake of her head.

Pixley sighed. The corridor running from the Mirror Room was long and narrow. He looked at what must be the room adjacent to the wall with the Napoleon painting. He jiggled the door handle. Blast it. Locked.

He put his ear against the door and listened. It was too thick to catch anything.

"May I help you, Mr Marsh?"

Pixley looked up. Marchesa Gloria's pencil-thin eyebrows were raised to her forehead.

"Ah, hello, Marchesa Gloria. It sounded like someone was crying inside. That's why I had my ear to the door."

"Crying? But who would be crying?"

"Is this a special room?"

"Gustavo!" she barked with surprising ferocity. "Gustavo!"

Gustavo lumbered toward them. "*Sì, Marchesa.*"

"Keys, Gustavo. Open this door." She smirked. "Mr Marsh heard someone crying."

Gustavo opened the door, revealing a small library. The cat darted inside.

Pixley shrugged. "I must've heard the cat."

"But the cat just went inside."

He heard heels clicking on the marble behind them.

Splendid! Ruby and Fina to the rescue.

Marchesa Gloria held out her hands as if she were greeting a long-lost relative. "So glad you're feeling better, Miss Dove. Are you sure you should be up and about?"

Pixley sighed with relief.

"Oh, yes. Right as rain," said Ruby, who had indeed made a miraculous recovery. Her hair and eyes shone. But Fina looked like she'd been attacked by a pair of nesting pigeons.

"We thought we'd find masks for the ball and then help you with your costume, Marchesa Gloria."

The white feathers lining Marchesa Gloria's robe-jacket quivered. "But yes! You must find your masks. I'll show you to the cellar and will tell you my costume plans along the way."

Sergio's head popped round the corner.

"Mr Marsh. We're waiting for you."

9

Fina twitched her nose. The cellar must be hundreds of years old. A musty, sour-wine odour. Must be the smell of wine bottles that had slipped to the floor, never arriving at the dinner table.

She gripped her candle-holder but the more she did, the more her light flickered.

"Sorry, sweeties. The cellar doesn't have electricity. It's positively ancient," said Marchesa Gloria, swinging around. Fina winced as bits of wax flew onto her face.

Oblivious, Marchesa Gloria continued. "Behold the magnificent masks." She pointed to long tables covered with white, pink, and black masks. "You may choose one to match your costume. What are you two going as?"

Ruby and Fina looked at one another. Before leaving Oxford, they'd had grand plans to sew magnificent costumes, but writing papers had come first. Fina sighed. Schoolwork always seemed to infringe on life.

"Our travel plans halted our costume plans, unfortunately," said Ruby. "But thankfully you have lovely masks." She ran her fingertip down a black silk mask.

"Not to worry, dearies." Marchesa Gloria opened an enormous chest and pulled out a frock patterned with red-and-green diamonds. Fina squealed. "It's scrumptious!"

Marchesa Gloria held up the frock to Fina. "You might need to let it out a bit." Fina turned red. Why did this woman dislike her so much?

The marchesa turned to Ruby. "If you sort through this chest, my dear, I'm sure you'll find something."

"What about your costume, Marchesa?" asked Ruby.

Marchesa Gloria's sky-blue eyes sparkled. "I plan to be Columbina, from the *Commedia dell'Arte* – the most popular Venetian costumes are from that play. Columbina is Harlequin's mistress, and often portrayed in rag-like clothing. But I want to be royal Columbina! And I'd prefer to be Lord Mayhew's mistress."

Ruby smiled. "Because we have so little time, I will take one of your gowns and fit the material around it. Light blue silk to match your eyes, I think."

Marchesa Gloria clapped her small hands together. "Perfect! I'll find a suitable gown." She took small, quick steps toward the stairs. She turned and blew Ruby a kiss.

"I cannot understand why I offend that woman," Fina said as soon as the door had closed.

"She's jealous."

"Of me? When donkeys will fly."

"Isn't it pigs?"

"What?"

"Isn't the expression when pigs will fly?"

"It's the Italian version."

"Impressive," mumbled Ruby as she bent down and rummaged through the costumes. "Yes. Don't you see? You almost look identical, except she has a double chin and fake blonde hair. And she's older than you."

Fina was settled in her insecurity about her appearance, so

she frowned. "I'd scarcely countenance it. Really?"

Ruby put a grotesque mask with a frown over her face and said in a deep voice, "Precisely."

Fina giggled. "Did you find a costume?"

The chest closed gently. "No. But I have an idea." She peered at the rows of masks and ran to the opposite end of the table. "Aha!" She held up an Egyptian goddess mask. "I'll go as Isis. I can picture her, but I cannot remember anything about her. Do you?"

"Isis. A wise goddess, a magician, and someone who put into action clever plots to fool her enemies. Her powers were used for healing and protection. Sounds exactly like you!"

"Splendid. I brought a figure-hugging red gown, which is precisely what she'd wear."

Fina pounced on a gold mask near her. She held it up and said "Meow!"

"Ah, you'll go as Gnaga, the cat woman. Though I heard men dressed as women in that costume. But it doesn't matter. It suits you."

"Did you hear that?" asked Fina.

"What?"

"Rattling. Like a stuck doorknob."

The cellar door opened and Fina jumped.

"Why are you so nervous?" asked Ruby. She called out, "Who's there?"

Silence.

Fina grabbed Ruby's arm as footsteps descended.

"WHERE THE DEVIL HAVE YOU BEEN?" hissed Sergio as Pixley slid back into the corridor.

"Call of nature, I'm afraid. Did I miss anything important?"

Sergio halted. "It was a snooze until you left. Then all hell broke loose."

Pixley's stomach fluttered, the way it fluttered every time he sniffed a news story. "Do tell."

Before Sergio could elaborate, a loud thud came from the Mirror Room.

They dashed into the meeting room, nearly colliding with Hazel Padmore.

"What a farrago," she muttered.

The scene was indeed a farrago. Papers floated amidst over-turned chairs. Emil scrambled on all fours, scooping up documents.

Lord Mayhew's normally placid face was twisted into a red gargoyle as he leaned over the table, propped up by his fists.

Opposite him stood Lady Asher, calm and collected. Only her mink looked distressed as he peeked over her shoulder at Pixley.

"If you think we'll cave in to a band of gangsters in the desert..." spluttered Mayhew.

"How about Mussolini? Is he not a gangster?" Lady Asher leaned over, her nose nearly touching Mayhew's. "All politics is organised crime by other means. To pretend otherwise is to be as naïve as a newborn babe."

Pixley's view of Lady Asher improved. Perhaps the old bird wasn't so bad.

Mayhew was apoplectic, though he stood his ground. "Then why are you involved in politics at all?"

Good point, thought Pixley.

"Because someone has to do something. Otherwise fools like you run the globe!" Then she murmured to herself, "I cannot understand why Gloria invited us all here."

Mayhew plopped down in his chair, clutching his chest. "Pills!" he croaked.

Emil's neatly stacked papers once again slid to the floor. He rummaged in Mayhew's coat pocket, finally locating a small silver tin, which he handed over. He then loosened Mayhew's tie as the man swallowed the pills.

Emil spread out his hands. "Lord Mayhew has a bad heart. He must have his pills."

Lady Asher snorted. "Shouldn't be running international negotiations if he might keel over dead at any moment." She flipped the mink's tail around her neck and marched off.

Sergio and Emil cooed over Mayhew like they were two nursemaids.

Pixley turned to Hazel, who sat near the door, looking profoundly disgusted.

"What the devil happened?" asked Pixley.

"Lady Asher suggested Britain should formally back Selassie as the rightful king. Then she went a step further and said Britain ought to publicly denounce Italy's invasion and demand their immediate withdrawal." Hazel ran her forefinger over one perfect eyebrow. "I disliked Lady Asher at first, but after that statement I've grown fond of her." She frowned.

"What's the matter, then?"

"It's just that something doesn't sit right. Lady Asher has never said any of these things publicly. In fact, she has avoided the topic even when questioned."

"I'll see you and raise you one. I remember her saying to the *Times* that England ought not get involved in any foreign affair, even if it were to help extricate the country from its overseas involvement."

"So why the change of heart?" asked Hazel.

"An unfortunate turn of phrase." Pixley pointed at Lord Mayhew.

Lord Mayhew's normally ruddy face had turned a translucent beige and he seemed to be gasping for breath. He rubbed his finger round the inside of his collar.

Even as they watched, Lord Mayhew's eyes slid shut, and he slumped awkwardly across the desk, out cold.

"Quick!" Ruby waved Fina behind the costume chest.

Fina gave Ruby a puzzled look. "Why are we hiding?" she whispered.

Voices interrupted Ruby's reply as they descended the stairs.

"It has been too long since that night in Paris, *tesora,*" said the male voice.

Fina scribbled in her tiny notebook, 'Magician. Il Grande Vittorio'.

A woman's voice came in return. "Much too long, *moya lyuba.* Though you've struck gold with your new assistant."

Fina scribbled 'Madam Zora' and showed Ruby the page.

Ruby goggled at Fina.

"What do you mean by that?" said Vittorio.

"You know very well what I mean by that," said Zora, parroting Il Grande's deep voice.

"She is but a child! A mere child. One must have a pretty assistant these days. No one wants to hire only a magician. Besides, her contortionist act brings a certain flair to my act. Times are hard, my Zora." Vittorio paused. "Come here."

Fina stuck out her tongue at Ruby in disgust. Then her nose twitched. She stared in horror at the specks of dust floating in the air. She held her hand over her nose, afraid to sneeze.

A table moved and Fina watched masks cascade to the floor. "You may not be interested in that young girl, but I saw your eyes on the marchesa. I am not stupid."

Ruby sneezed.

They froze.

Silence was followed by rapid footfall.

"Is this your latest trick, young ladies?"

Il Grande's gleaming teeth shone as he peered over the chest.

Fina's knees wouldn't move.

Ruby popped up like a jack-in-the-box. "A few costumes fell behind the chest." She held up Fina's gown as evidence. "And then we heard you... and realised you must want to be alone. So we weren't keen on disturbing a lovers' scene."

Fina nodded, though she still could not get up.

"We are not lovers." Madam Zora thumped what appeared to be a decorative cane. She had changed into a long-sleeved black velvet gown with a high neck and emerald brooch at the throat.

"Oh, I just assumed."

Vittorio smoothed his hair. "We were discussing business arrangements."

"Of course." Ruby helped Fina to her feet.

Madam Zora blinked. "I forgot myself. You are Ruby Dove! I am glad you are mended."

Vittorio kissed Ruby's hand.

"But we must talk. Now!" cried Madam Zora. "I have many questions for you. So many questions."

With tiny quick steps, Zora grabbed Ruby's hand and led her up the stairs. Ruby glanced back at Fina and smiled with pleasure.

Fina nodded and scooped up the fallen masks. "Have you selected your costume, Vittorio?"

There was that all-too-charming grin again, emphasized by the wrinkles round his eyes and his sharp white teeth. "My dear, I am too famous to dress up as someone else. If you are famous yourself, why not go as yourself?"

Selkies and kelpies. "But surely you'll need a mask." She playfully held up her cat mask.

He held up a white *bauta* mask, leaving only his brown eyes visible. "You play innocent, but you cannot fool me, you little minx." His cape billowed out behind him as he approached, the smell of hair oil wafting around him.

Fina stepped backward once, twice, three times, until her back was against the wall. "Please. You must have me mixed up with someone else. I am quite innocent. What you see is what you get."

"I'll stop your adorable babbling." He took a step closer. "With a kiss."

Should she scream?

"Help!" she cried.

"No one can hear you, my sweet."

She spied a metal pole propped against the wall. Before Vittorio could pin her against the wall, she grabbed the pole and brought it down hard against his gleaming forehead.

Fina would never forget the 'crack' sound as the pole brought Vittorio to his knees and then to the ground. The pole clanged as she let it fall to the floor. He lay still, arms rigid at his sides.

His chest stopped moving with his breath. Fina held hers as she felt for his pulse, but there was not even a flutter of life.

Pursing her lips over an impending scream crawling up her throat, she hopped over his body and dashed up the stairs, gasping for breath as she pushed the cellar door open.

10

Blinded by tears, Fina stumbled into the lighted hallway. She leaned against the banister and then reeled back, queasy.

Pixley trundled toward her, huffing and puffing. "Feens! We need a doctor! Mayhew is unconscious."

She blinked, temporarily diverted. "Gustavo knows about medicine. Let's find him."

"Right. We'll split up—"

"No, Pixley. We need to talk."

"Splendid, Feens. We'll have a chinwag soon. Half a tick, until we find good old Gustavo." He stopped, his eyes wide. "You've been crying. What's the matter?"

Fina's stomach clenched as she wiped her eyes with her sleeve, not caring that her mother would be mortified by this slovenly act. "You're right. We need to find a doctor. I'll tell you later."

He set off at a trot toward the bedrooms. Fina tried to keep up. As they rounded the corner, she bumped into Isa Fiore. Though their bodies hit each other, Isa's immediately melted away like an apparition.

"Ah, *scusi.*" She was wrapped in an aubergine silk dressing-gown, with a towel around her neck. The moment she saw Fina, she snatched up the towel and began winding it around her head, squeezing it as if to dry her hair. Odd. Her blonde curls had looked fluffy and light, and there were no droplets on her dressing-gown. Fina opened her mouth to speak, but Isa cut in quickly. "Have you seen Vittorio? I've been searching for him everywhere."

Struggling to concentrate, Fina blurted, "He's a magician. Maybe he's working on a disappearing trick."

Isa snorted and twirled her dressing-gown sash. "Amusing, Miss Aubrey-Havelock, but I assure you he's not working on a trick. We were supposed to meet twenty minutes ago. He is never late – I am the one who is always tardy!"

A bead of sweat tickled Fina's neck. "Must dash. Lord Mayhew is poorly. Do you have any medical training, by any chance?"

"A little. My mother taught me because she was a nurse in the war. Where is Mayhew?"

"Thank goodness. Mayhew's in the large room at the end of the hall. Please hurry!"

Fina watched as Isa performed her version of a run. She ran like the sugar-plum fairy.

As she turned back, Fina spied Pixley and Ruby emerging from Madam Zora's room.

"Ruby!" she cried, as Madam Zora also stepped into the corridor.

Zora smiled. "Do you always greet your friends with such passion? Perhaps you are secretly Italian, Miss Aubrey-Havelock."

With a flaming-hot face, Fina said, "Please excuse me, Madam Zora. Lord Mayhew has been taken ill and I found a nurse to help him – Isa Fiore – which is why I became rather agitated."

"What's the matter with Lord Mayhew?" asked Ruby.

"Jiffy heart is my diagnosis," said Pixley. "The man's a natural apoplectic – bound to keel over one day from a piffling disagreement." He paused. "Sorry. That sounded harsh. I'm glad you found Isa because I cannot find Gustavo."

"He's in the cellar," said Ruby.

Fina's heart stopped.

"What do you mean, in the cellar?" she asked.

Ruby stared at her. "After he left refreshments for us in Madam Zora's room, he said he must check on the wine selection for tonight's meal."

Fina steadied herself on Pixley's arm, wondering how on earth she could get rid of Madam Zora.

In an attempt to calm her shattered nerves, she forced herself to focus on Zora's clothes. They were certainly worth looking at. Simple, clean lines with a splash of the unusual. Zora herself was clad in a long grey gown with a navy hood and a smooth emerald ring.

"I've never seen a hood in high fashion before," said Fina.

Zora's eyes twinkled. "My creations are magnificent, if I say so myself. And we've already planned Ruby's Isis frock out of the same material I used for Mr Pixley's favourite red jumper."

Pixley jiggled his leg. "Red jumper? Did you say red jumper?"

"But yes, of course." Zora pulled out the magical piece of clothing from her wardrobe and handed it to Pixley.

Pixley gawped. "I–I–I don't know what to say." He ran a finger up and down the garment.

"You're never at a loss for words, Pix," laughed Ruby. "It's most kind of you, but I'm afraid we must leave."

"So soon? We have so much more to discuss!"

"Yes, I'm concerned about Fina. She ought to lie down."

"WHAT'S THE MATTER, FEENS?" hissed Pixley.

"I tried to tell you earlier, but you wouldn't listen," pouted Fina when they were safely in Pixley's room.

"Hmmm?" Pixley stared lovingly at his red jumper.

"He's been lost to the world of the red jumper. Ignore him," said Ruby. "Tell me what happened."

Fina sank into a soft armchair and poured out her tragic story. Even Pixley listened.

"So you see, Gustavo probably found the body and now they'll think I murdered Vittorio!" Fina rose and paced around the armchair.

Ruby grabbed her arm. "Pacing only makes you more agitated. I've seen it before, so why don't you sit down?"

Fina crumpled into an armchair and buried her face in her hands. "They'll arrest me, I'll go to jail and then... do they have hanging in Italy?"

Pixley pulled Fina's hands from her face. "Stay calm, Fina. Everything will be fine. Ruby and I would never let anything happen to you. You could always say you were defending yourself against the swine. Perhaps you thought you killed him—"

"The sound was so loud."

"Pixley's right. You might have knocked him unconscious."

Fina shook her head. "I'm certain I killed him."

"Why do you say that?" asked Ruby.

"Because I stayed long enough to check his pulse. It had stopped."

11

Pixley switched on the cellar light.

"That's peculiar," said Fina. "I'd left it on."

"Gustavo must have turned it off," said Ruby.

Fina gripped the cool railing. "After he discovered Il Grande's body. Why hasn't there been an uproar?"

"Maybe he overlooked it," said Pixley.

Fina glared at Pixley.

"Just trying to be optimistic," he said.

As they descended the stairs, Fina shuddered at the mask-covered tables. Before, they had looked inviting and intriguing. Now, they were frightening reminders of her encounter with Vittorio. Everything was quiet, and nothing looked out of place.

"Where's Vittorio?" asked Pixley.

Fina stared at the pole on the floor, in the exact position she'd left it.

Ruby bent over and picked something up. "Does this help?"

She handed a black thread to Fina.

"I suppose it could be from his cape," she said. "But it doesn't explain what happened to his cape, or to his body."

Pixley sighed. "Maybe you imagined it all – you do have a fertile imagination."

Fina spun round, eyes narrowed. "Pixley Hayford..."

Ruby covered Pixley's mouth with her hand. "Pay no attention to his comments – he's just regurgitating things he's learned elsewhere."

Pixley gently removed Ruby's hand. "Sorry. That was uncalled for. My apologies."

Fina crouched down, wiping away dust on the floor as if on an archaeological dig. "He must have left something behind – he can't have just disappeared." She straightened up. "Do you think Gustavo discovered the body and dragged it upstairs without telling anyone?"

Ruby shrugged. "It's possible, but seems unlikely. Why would he go to all that trouble, when he'd be more likely to call the police, or at least consult with Marchesa Gloria?"

Pixley sneezed. "The dust is getting to me, so I'll toddle off upstairs."

Fina grabbed his arm. "Don't leave us, Pix."

"Don't worry. I'll stand sentry like a Roman bodyguard with my mask, in case anyone dares to question me." He grabbed a terrifying white *bauta* mask and sprang up the stairs.

"Perhaps we ought to follow him." Ruby leaned the pole Fina had used against the wall. "There isn't a trace of anything on the pole."

"Are you saying you don't believe me? That I'm a fantasist?"

She heard a cough from above and looked up. Pixley was cleaning his spectacles with a handkerchief. "I've returned, dear ladies. I'm afraid someone has locked us in."

"Curse this cellar," fumed Fina. "Curse all cellars, especially ones with wine vats," she added, remembering their first adventure in Italy, or rather, Sardinia.

"I agree," said Pixley. "I'd much prefer to be stuck on a train in the Alps."

The air suddenly seemed to thin, causing Fina to catch her breath. "Will we run out of oxygen?"

Ruby clicked her tongue. "No time to become maudlin, children. Where's your fighting spirit? There must be a way out of here."

Fina snorted. "What, you mean a secret passage? That only happens in detective stories, Ruby."

Ruby silently drew her fingertips over the cracks in the cobblestone wall.

Pixley mimicked Ruby's tracing pattern on the opposite wall. "She's been feeding you banana oil, Feens. I believe you were in the corridor when Marchesa Gloria mentioned something about secret passages."

Fina crossed her arms. "Selkies and kelpies, no one tells me anything." She stamped her left foot on the stone tile so hard it sent a shooting pain into her ankle.

"What's that scraping noise?" asked Pixley.

"It's coming from the corner." Ruby pointed to a small recess as she rushed over. "It's a secret passage – good work, Feens!"

"At least her temper is useful sometimes," murmured Pixley.

"I heard that, Mr Hayford," Fina said in an uncontrollable giggle. She rushed behind Ruby, popping her head round her into the gloom and brushing away a cobweb from Ruby's hair. "How will we see without torches?"

Ruby tapped her teeth. "Pix, do you still have your pipe?"

Pixley patted his blazer pockets. "I prefer cigarettes, so I mostly use it as a good journalist prop." He pulled an elegant rosewood pipe from his breast pocket. "But the pipe's glow wouldn't even let a mouse find its way through that darkness."

"I have an idea. Skis."

Pixley and Fina glanced at each other. With worry. She hadn't seen any skis.

Ruby waved them on. "Follow me." She pointed at a slip of paper reading 'skis', pinned on a red door.

"Well, I'll be gobsmacked!" cried Pixley. His grin turned to a frown. "But why do we need skis?"

The top half of Ruby's body had disappeared into the cupboard. She emerged with a silver tube covered with a blue label. "Ski wax!"

"What's ski wax?" asked Fina, feeling like an unsophisticated country mouse.

To her relief, Pixley said, "Yes, what in God's name is ski wax?"

"You rub it on the bottom of your skis so clumps of snow don't stick to them, slowing you down."

"Ruby Dove, I love you, but sometimes your expertise in everything is maddening," sighed Pixley.

"Everything?" she responded with a tinkling laugh. "Scarcely everything. I'm rather a dunce when it comes to languages, for example. That's Fina's department."

Fina shivered, suddenly remembering their predicament and what she had done to Vittorio. "Tell us how to use the wax. Were you thinking of using it as a candle?"

"Precisely. Although if we light the wax in this flimsy tube, I'm afraid it will get too hot. Here." She handed the tube to Pixley. "Scoop out the wax – it's much softer than candle wax – and put it into your pipe."

"And ruin a perfectly good pipe? Not on your life!"

Fina put a hand on Pixley's arm. "I'm sure we can clean the pipe once we're through. It will probably work better than ever – besides, do we have a choice?"

Like a man resigned to the gallows, Pixley plopped down in a nearby chair and began to scoop out the wax. He grimaced. "It's sticky and gooey."

"Aren't men supposed to trudge through sleet and snow for their women?" Ruby grinned.

"I don't go in for rubbish masculinity."

Ruby pulled out a tiny pair of scissors from one of her hidden pockets and snipped away the string from a nearby black mask. Then she snipped the string into many pieces, handing one to Pixley. "Stick one of these into the pipe to make a wick. I'll carry the others if our makeshift candle doesn't last long enough."

Pixley did as he was told and lit the wick. The pipe-candle glowed.

Fina clapped her hands. "Spiffing work, Ruby. Now let's get out of here!"

12

"Listen." Pixley brushed a cobweb from his forehead. "Sounds like running water."

Fina glanced up the tunnel stairs and listened. The running water stopped. "There's a lavatory near the ground-floor cellar door. Maybe that's what we heard." She pulled a silken cape she'd found in a costume trunk around her more tightly. Her breath was visible in the glow from Pixley's pipe.

Ruby squeezed Fina's hand. She whispered, "I'm still afraid of the dark."

Pixley spun round. The candle flickered and nearly blew out. "What?"

Through gritted teeth, Ruby said, "I'm afraid of the dark."

"But we've wandered in darkness before on our cases – literally and metaphorically. Why now?" asked Pixley.

"I never outgrew the childhood fear, so I tried hypnosis and it worked. Perhaps it wore off."

"Hypnosis? But you're so scientific – isn't it hocus pocus?" asked Fina.

Ruby sighed. "Hypnosis is scientific."

Pixley handed Ruby the pipe. "Here, you can lead us with my pipe – you'll feel more secure if you're in control."

With a smile and a shaking hand, Ruby took the pipe and advanced toward the uneven staircase.

Fina plunged forward after her, her foot stepping on something that made a crinkling noise. "Ruby, would you shine a light here?" Fina bent down and picked up two paper bags. They were creased and crumpled but empty.

"They're not covered in dust, so they must have been left here recently."

"Damned if I know what it means." Pixley turned to Ruby. She shrugged.

Pixley shivered. "Better put them down... there's probably a giant spider lurking inside."

Ruby brushed off her shoulders. "Don't mention spiders, Pixley Hayford!"

The bags floated to the floor as Fina rushed upward after Ruby and Pixley. At the top of the stairs, the passage levelled out into a cobwebbed corridor. Fina picked her way along, nearly tripping over a loose stone tile. As she grasped the wall for support, her fingers touched something jutting out. It was a flat metal bar, so she tugged at it this way and that, finally pulling it down on its hinges. A squeaking, creaking noise came from inside the wall and two narrow streams of light illuminated the tunnel.

Pixley and Ruby backtracked, eyes wide. "What did you do?" asked Ruby.

"I accidentally found this lever and pulled it." Pixley peered into the two holes.

"By Jove, it's Napoleon!" He did a little jig. "Have I ever told you you're a genius, Red?"

"Not lately, no," laughed Fina. "But why Napoleon? Is the little man your role model?"

"Hilarious, dear Fina," came Pixley's muffled voice as his face pressed against the wall. "Earlier, while you two were gallivanting about, I was engaged in serious negotiations with Lord Mayhew, Lady Asher, Hazel Padmore, Emil Pleischner, and Sergio Chapman. While Lord Mayhew droned on about something-or-other, I had a jolly good look around: bored faces, Ming vases, plush rugs, and paintings. But then, the Napoleon portrait's eyes moved. I remember wiping my spectacles and counting the glasses of wine I'd drunk at lunch. When I stared at the devious cove again, he had eyes of the human variety, not the oil-paint kind. I made my excuses to leave and tried to enter the room where I thought the painting would be, only to be waylaid by Marchesa Gloria."

"It's possible there are multiple peephole-paintings," said Ruby. "Though I suppose we might be parallel to the Mirror Room."

"Who would know of the secret passage, much less this spyhole?" asked Fina.

"Let's discuss this once we've escaped this blasted tunnel. Hurry." Pixley dashed further into the darkness, without his flickering pipe.

"He'll hurt himself," said Fina. "Why is he rushing?"

Ruby grabbed Fina's arm and pushed her forward. "Because there was a flash of light. Someone's coming."

Fina stared at the empty chair at the long oval dinner table. Antipasti dishes littered the surface, scattered about like a seventeenth-century still-life painting. Cheerful murmurs and little laughs floated across to her, the contented atmosphere only enhancing Fina's sense of doom. A nearby dish with olive pits caused self-pitying tears to well up.

Daria stacked plates onto a nearby wooden cart while Gustavo served the *primo* dishes. "And now, we have *risotto con pesce persico.*" He placed a white risotto platter with pale pan-fried fish in front of them.

Emil leaned over. "What might that be, Miss Aubrey-Havelock?"

"Local fresh fish over risotto." She sniffed and wiped her eyes. "But I thought you spoke Italian, Mr Pleischner."

"Emil, please. Yes, I speak the Italian – oh dear, my languages are becoming mixed up in my head. Now I am having trouble with English."

Fina grabbed a nearby bottle of wine and poured a healthy dose into Emil's empty glass. "Here, this ought to help. My spoken German is dreadful, otherwise I'd give it a go."

Emil smiled and sipped the red wine, making a smacking noise like a sommelier. "Delicious. Grumello – a local wine. Or nearly local."

"See, you're already more relaxed." Fina hoisted her glass and clinked it against Emil's. "Now, what was this about the fish?"

"I have allergies to cheese – mostly to parmesan. Does the dish contain parmesan?"

"It has sage, wine, and a bit of butter." She scrunched up her face. "Yes, yes, it has parmesan."

Emil's face fell. "What a pity."

"But this dish, *brasato di cinghiale selvatico*, is wild boar with wine and vegetables." Fina pointed at large chunks of meat covered in a reddish-brown sauce.

Rubbing his hands together, Emil tucked his napkin into his collar and gripped his knife and fork in each hand, as if they might slip away. Fina smiled despite herself at someone who enjoyed food as much as she did, though tonight she formed the risotto into little piles on her plate.

"You are not hungry?" Emil swallowed his first bite.

"I'm worried about someone."

"Surely it is not Lord Mayhew – he is quite fit now." Emil motioned to the red-faced Mayhew, chortling over what could only be a bawdy joke told by the marchesa. She had already impressed them with her command of inappropriate anatomical references during the cocktail hour.

Emil sliced a chunk of meat into two perfect halves. "No, Lord Mayhew has recovered after this afternoon. I've seen it happen to him before – it looks like a heart attack, but it's actually a fainting spell."

"I've never heard of men having fainting spells before," said Fina in a wry voice.

The irony was lost on Emil. "*Ja*, men have them, too. Though it is odd more men do not have them, as women are stronger. *Meine Frau...*" He waved his fork about, causing sauce to splatter across the white tablecloth. A flash of disapproval crossed Hazel's impassive face, momentarily covered by her dabbing the corners of her mouth.

"Have you travelled much, Miss Padmore?" Fina started another conversation, hoping it would distract her further.

"A great deal – I become restless if I don't keep moving. I've travelled to Ethiopia, Egypt, India, China, and all over Europe. My favourite location, though, is the Caribbean. I have relatives in the Bahamas who keep a room ready for me. I'd love to live there someday."

"What keeps you in London?"

"Politics, of course. There is so much to be done to organise pan-African interests, and London is really the best location, given its proximity to world power. But I often travel to the Bahamas to visit my uncle and auntie."

Ruby's longtime on-again-off-again boyfriend, Ian Clavering, was also from the Bahamas. Asking someone if they knew someone else just because they lived in the same country was a longtime pet peeve of Fina's, but her curiosity drove her on.

"I don't suppose you've met a man called Ian Clavering?" It was a long shot, but why not distract herself?

"Ian!" Hazel squeaked, suddenly transforming into a twelve-year-old schoolgirl. Her normally placid arms waved about. "But how delightful. How did you meet Ian Clavering?"

Pixley glanced over, momentarily diverted from his chat with Sergio. He was glowing, either from his red jumper – definitely his colour – or from the intensity of their conversation. "So you know Ian Clavering. Well, well, well. Won't Ruby be pleased." He eyed Ruby, who sat next to Marchesa Gloria, oblivious to their conversation. Pixley pushed his spectacles higher. "Do tell. How did you meet?"

Hazel cast her eyes down. "We met at a social for African students in London – last December, I believe. He told me about his theatre productions and future plans. We had a kiss under the mistletoe." She giggled. "He's a charmer."

"That he is," said Fina, grimly.

Hazel looked from Pixley to Fina. "How did you meet?"

"We—" said Pixley and Fina in unison.

Fina held up a hand, much preferring whatever explanation Pixley would dream up. She didn't want to explain how they'd first met Ian last December as well – over a corpse. And she certainly didn't want to say anything about Ruby's relationship.

"I visited Ruby and Fina in Oxford for a story, and he happened to be there visiting a friend of his. A male friend." Pixley sipped his wine and began to choke. He threw down his napkin and ran out, but not before he made a slight nod at Fina.

"Would you excuse me?" Fina followed, aware of Ruby's eyes tracking her every step.

In the corridor, Pixley paced, his hands in the tiny side-slit pockets of his red jumper. "Feens, is something going on between Hazel and Ian?"

"She said they kissed."

"It might have been innocent – I've kissed my grandmother under the mistletoe before."

"True. And she said he was a charmer, which could imply she knows not to fall for his charms."

"I'll wring his neck if he's leading Ruby on," fumed Pixley.

"Leading Ruby on to what?" asked Ruby.

R<small>UBY'S</small> backlit silhouette glowed angelically in the corridor, making it even more difficult to lie. Which Fina intended to do.

Pixley ran a finger round his collar. "Ah, Ruby. We were discussing whether Madam Zora led you on."

"Madam Zora? But you said 'he'." Ruby took one step closer.

"You must have misheard," put in Fina. "We were worried Madam Zora would take you under her wing and then drop you like a hot potato."

Ruby took another step closer. "But why would she do that? She altered one of her divine gowns for me to wear tonight."

It was indeed divine. Zora's signature long sleeves and high collar in a muted green velvet looked positively medieval, save a daring cutout in the back.

"These artistic types are notoriously unstable," said Pixley. "One minute they love you, then they flit toward another shiny object. Much like a magpie."

Ruby hung her head. "Like Ian, you mean."

Pixley and Fina rushed to Ruby's side. "Ian loves you. It's clear to anyone who's in your company, Ruby," said Fina softly, thinking dreamily of her own flighty Idris. "He adores you, but his work takes him away. And you have to admit, you'd scarcely want to be tied down anywhere, much less get married."

Ruby's eyes turned glassy. "Perhaps you're right. I'm always cross with him for leaving, but if he stuck to me like a limpet, I'd be irritated."

"There now." Pixley rubbed Fina's arm like he was her grandfather. "Fina's hit it. The three of us are adventurers, unwilling to be tied down. Though a little romantic intrigue wouldn't go amiss," he sighed.

Ruby brightened. "Dear Pix, I do believe you're smitten. Tell us who it is, right now."

Pixley sighed. "Well, the elegant Hazel is out of my league, as they say, but someone has shown interest as of late."

Fina pulled on his sleeve like a small child, though she knew full well who it was. "Tell us, Pix, tell us now!"

"What's all the racket about, children?" Sergio popped his head round the door. Hazel followed, lurking behind.

Sergio waved his cigarette. "Am I missing the real party? Dear Pix, we must finish our conversation – I want to hear what the Duchess of Perthshire said about her shaved cat."

Pixley grinned, like a shaved Cheshire cat.

13

The next day, Fina and Ruby dashed about, fitting up Marchesa Gloria's costume, sewing their own, and laughing over their costume for Pixley.

Pixley spent the day grazing on various delights in the Mirror Room. In between sessions, he'd chat with Sergio about legal possibilities for international actions against the Italian government. Much to his relief, Napoleon did not make eyes at him, though Sergio certainly did.

As the ball drew near, Fina's stomach knots tightened. No one mentioned Vittorio's absence. It was as if he'd never existed. Finally, as she and Zora put the final touches on Ruby's Isis costume – with Ruby encased in a tight cherry-red gown – she mustered up the courage.

"Mhhdfdsfds..." said Fina.

"What's that, dear? Here, let me take those pins from your mouth." Zora extricated a mass of pins from between Fina's lips, but they fell to the floor. Fina noticed the designer's finger joints looked swollen.

"Sorry. It's peculiar Vittorio wasn't at dinner last night. Apparently he hasn't been seen since."

"Isa Fiore said he'd had urgent business across the lake – an ill aunt," said Madam Zora.

Though Zora had instructed Ruby not to move an inch, she rolled her eyes at Fina.

"That's odd, since Isa said she didn't know his whereabouts," said Fina.

"She said he'd return for the ball tonight, so I have no reason to doubt her veracity." She paused, eyes twinkling. "Do you, dear Fina?"

"Oh, no," she mumbled. "Ruby and Pixley call me Red the Inquisitor – I've always had difficulty restraining my curiosity."

The twinkle in Zora's eyes disappeared. "I'm sure I know about cats and curiosity – one of the few English idioms I know. The Duchess of Perthshire taught it to me."

A knock came at the door.

"It must be Pixley," said Ruby. "I told him to come for a costume-fitting when the negotiations finished."

As Ruby opened the door, Fina's mouth hung open. She'd expected a tired and somewhat cranky Pixley. Instead, a glowing god stood in the doorway.

Zora peered at Pixley's pores as if she were a dermatologist. "Mr Marsh – Pixley – whatever have you put on your skin? I must have your night cream recipe."

Pixley pursed his lips as if he prevented himself from blurting out an impertinence. Then he said calmly, "It must be the cold – Sergio and I just had a bracing garden stroll."

Ruby winked at Fina.

"Come, come, Pixley. It's time for your costume-fitting!" said Zora.

"Fantastic. But I don't want to take off my red jumper." He rubbed it lovingly. Fina wouldn't have been surprised if he'd slept in it.

"While I'm flattered, dear heart, you'll be most pleased with

Ruby and Fina's concoction." Zora sat down in a Louis XIV chair and sipped her tea. "I'll watch, though I'm too thrilled to sit still."

Pixley looked scandalised by the 'I'll watch' statement, but shrugged and took off his jacket and coat.

Ruby clicked her tongue. "Your trousers are too bulky."

He held up his forefinger. "Never fear!" Pixley disappeared behind a gold-and-silver changing screen. He emerged in woollen long underwear, such as one wears for skiing.

Zora, Ruby, and Fina broke out into fits of laughter.

Pixley looked down at his clothing, bewildered. "What's the matter, haven't you ever seen long johns before?"

Fina wiped her eyes. "Yes, but not someone wearing it indoors. Have you been wearing that all day? You must have been roasting during the negotiations!"

He crossed his arms. "I'll have you know I was perfectly snug as a bug in a rug. While everyone else was shivering in that blasted room – the fireplace doesn't heat it very well – I was quite comfortable." Pixley tapped his foot. "Are you going to laugh at me all day or shall I behold this magnificent costume?"

"Yes, Your Highness," said Ruby. "But you must shut your eyes while Fina and I help you into the costume. Then you can peek."

"The things I put up with," he sighed, waving his spectacles in Zora's direction.

"Yes, you are a saint, Mr Marsh." Zora smiled.

"At least someone appreciates me around here." He set down his spectacles, closed his eyes and held his arms out.

As Fina pulled up a sleeve, she whispered, "So who is it? Hazel or Sergio?"

"Dear Hazel is rather hot and cold on me. Her loss. No, I've turned my attentions to Sergio, someone who seems to appreciate me."

"Well, it certainly has done wonders for your complexion – not that it was bad before."

"Thank you, Red. Can I open my eyes now to see this blasted costume?"

In a normal voice, Ruby said, "Almost. But we must put on your mask."

They lowered the mask onto his face and tied the strap around the back of his head.

Ruby waved her hand at a large looking-glass. "Ta-da! Behold!"

Pixley gasped. "What the devil?"

Once more, they all broke into fits of giggles, save Pixley, who removed the grotesque beaked mask and threw it down.

"You have me pegged as Pulcinella? The ugly one from *Commedia dell'Arte,* with the hunchback?"

They had constructed a marvellous hunchback with a pillow and a bit of string.

Ruby rubbed his arm soothingly. "Hush now, Pix. It's just a joke. We wanted to see how you'd react, but we'd never think of you as Pulcinella, especially now you have one – or perhaps two – people to impress."

Zora put in, "I've never seen someone give Pulcinella such flair before. Impressive, Mr Marsh." She winked at Fina.

Pixley's shoulders lowered. "Sorry. I'm a little more fussy about my appearance given, well, the circs. You understand."

"But you shall go to the ball!" Fina waved a yardstick like a magic wand.

"Yes, Fairy Godmother, I shall. But I haven't a stitch to wear." With a sigh, Pixley looked at the clock. "It's almost 9pm and I'll turn into a pumpkin in a half-hour if you don't get me into the right costume soon."

Ruby turned round, clad in a blue-and-silver leather mask.

"It's Khonsu, Egyptian god of the moon. That's your role tonight."

Pixley grinned. "Spiffing. Though those gods often go bare-chested, and I'm not prepared for that, especially in this weather."

"We have gauze-like material that matches your skin colour, and a wrap for your bottom half. The only other piece besides the neck-gear is his side lock." Fina held up the costume.

"Side lock?" Pixley's face fell.

"We've cut a wig in half, so it will be perfect, especially since you're bald anyway," said Ruby.

Zora set down her teacup and rose. "Children, I'm afraid the fun is over, at least while I need to go and dress in my own costume before this night of debauchery."

Pixley, Ruby, and Fina murmured profuse apologies, gathered up their belongings and dashed into the hallway. A tall, masked man approached them, carrying a tray of empty drinks glasses. Peculiar how one small strip of black leather could so alter one's appearance, thought Fina. It must be Gustavo.

He nodded at them and marched away.

"Let's change in my room," said Ruby. "It's the largest and I have two changing screens."

As they turned into Ruby's room, an elfin, troll-like character limped toward them, clad in green-and-brown felt. The enormous ears and long nose defeated Fina's attempts at recognition.

The creature grunted and half-ran, half-limped toward the stairs.

Fina jumped.

Pixley tapped her on the arm. "Pssst... Feens. No need to jump – everyone's in costume, remember?"

"Stop teasing her, Pix." Ruby opened her bedroom door. "You'd be jumpy, too, if you cracked someone over the head, thought they were dead, and then disappeared."

"True. A playfully mischievous mood gripped me."

Fina couldn't help herself. "More like you were gripped by love."

"Touché. We're even now," he grinned.

"Look!" cried Fina. "Someone's left a bottle of bubbly. How thoughtful, especially because I need to calm my nerves."

Ruby's delighted eyes narrowed. "Is it open? Why would someone leave a bottle of champagne, especially if it could get warm?"

The cork popped as Pixley gripped the bottle, sending him scooching backward, narrowly missing the volcanic foam. "Nope. Good as new and nothing to worry about. Bottoms up!"

As the golden liquid slid down her throat, Fina heard a far-off rumble. "Did you hear that?"

Pixley set down his glass. "Sounded like a herd of elephants."

"It's coming from downstairs," said Fina.

"Perhaps Lady Asher has recruited all the guests to march about like her."

"Hilarious, Pix." Ruby grabbed her silver wrap. "But we'd better see what's wrong."

14

When the trio rushed down the stairs, the solution to the elephant mystery was revealed.

A twenty-person band blared jazz at the far end of the ballroom. The main source of the elephantine rumble was the drummer: a tiny, wiry man in a white suit. The band struck up *Merry Go Round*, sending the costumed guests whirling about in a frenzy. The long ballroom gleamed from low-hanging crystal chandeliers reflecting on the black-and-white marble floor. Gustavo stood behind a makeshift bar, frantically pouring cocktails. A tall nun served canapés. Strands of blonde hair escaped her habit, signalling it must be Daria. Only two other servers worked the crowd: a priest and a devil. Fina wondered why they continued to be so short-staffed, especially if Marchesa Gloria could afford to put on such a grand ball. Guests packed the room, most likely the elite of Bellagio and Lake Como, judging by the fantastic jewels around the ladies' necks and the occasional robin's-egg-sized rings on their fingers.

Pixley tapped his foot and began to sway. Fina smiled as she realised Pixley had to dance in a long, tight skirt. Harlequin sidled up with a side-stepping motion and tapped Pixley on the shoulder. He lifted his mask and whispered into Pixley's ear.

Ruby leaned over in her tight-fitting red Isis costume, her long earring hitting Fina in the face. "Sorry, Feens! Do you think Harlequin is Sergio?"

"Most definitely, given how quickly he buttonholed Pix." Fina grimaced. "Won't it cause a scene? Two men dancing together?"

Ruby's wry smile disappeared as she sipped her martini. "I doubt if anyone cares about anything as dull as propriety at this masquerade, my straight-laced friend."

Fina stamped her foot, causing a donkey to turn round in surprise. She ignored the Eeyore look from the mask and said, "I'm not straight-laced. You're the one who's Miss Prim and Proper." As soon as she uttered the phrase, her stomach clenched. "What came over me? I'm so sorry. I didn't mean it, dear Ruby."

Ruby waved her martini glass. "Perfectly normal reaction, Red, given the circs, as Pix would say."

Irrationally, Fina felt annoyed that Ruby wouldn't even get mad at her for insulting her.

"Why don't you ever get mad at me? Or even irritated. The most I've ever seen you become is exasperated."

"Are you trying to pick a fight?"

"See? Even that is a rational reaction."

"What is rational, darling?" came a voice. "Irrationality is more delightful!"

Ruby and Fina turned round. Though the iridescent blue-green dragonfly's face was masked, the fluttering arms could only belong to one person. Iveta.

"*Mi chiamo Iveta Da Silva*," she said, her wings quivering as she bowed.

Fina set down her drink. "It's us, Iveta. Fina and Ruby."

"Your costumes are magnificent! Dear Ruby, let me guess.

You are Isis, the Egyptian goddess, and Fina, you are Gnaga, the cat woman. Though I thought men were supposed to dress as Gnaga as a woman?"

For once, Fina's red face was hidden. She felt grateful for the Gnaga mask. "I'm a cat aficionado, so I had to dress as one."

"But of course, precious. I brought this dragonfly costume with me from Rio – it's tragic to miss Carnival this year, but this party is much better than I imagined. So much intrigue!"

Ruby leaned forward, eyes gleaming. "What intrigue?"

Iveta wagged her finger. "Naughty, naughty, my gemstone. I see your eyes like a bloodhound on the scent, though there is no murder this time."

Sergio and Pixley joined them. "Pixley's an excellent dancer. Good show all around from the marchesa. I wonder when the old man will perform?"

"Old man?" asked Pixley.

"You know, the great magician. Come on, let's have another twirl on the floor, shall we?"

Inexplicably, fingers of anxiety crept up around Fina's shoulders. "Would you excuse me?" She looked at Ruby and Iveta. "I'm sure you two have much to discuss."

Ruby tugged on Fina's sleeve and whispered, "Sorry. Do you forgive me for our spat?"

She said nothing but nodded, dashing into the corridor. Leaning against a tall marble column, Fina removed her mask and gulped in the fresh air.

"Too much party for you as well, I see," said a voice behind the column. A head poked round. Or rather a skull, smoking a cigarette.

Fina jumped, pulling her mask back down over her face. "You startled me, especially with your fabulous costume."

The skeleton leaned against the column, one leg crossed.

Whoever it was inside had a British accent, but it was strangely neutral in affect and tone.

"Who are you?" queried the ever-direct Fina.

With a little snort, the skeleton replied, "I believe that's not playing the game, my dear Gnaga. You only reveal yourself at midnight – or am I mixing it up with a Victory Ball?"

"Are you a guest?"

"Of sorts. I'm here to settle a few scores."

A gaggle of medieval musicians traipsed past them, momentarily diverting Fina with their chatter and colourful costumes. When she looked back, the skeleton had vanished.

"Is that you, Fina?"

A white-masked figure in a tiered white frock speckled with gold stars tapped Fina on the shoulder. Though the top half of the body faced Fina, the bottom half faced the ballroom archway.

"Yes, it's Fina. And you must be Isa. What's your costume?"

"But how did you recognise me?" breathed Isa through the small mouth-hole in her mask.

"You're twisted like a contortionist!"

"Ah!" She laughed through her nose. "It's so natural, I don't even notice it. As for my costume, I'm Pierrette, from *Commedia dell'Arte*. She's Piero's star-crossed lover – an excellent costume for a woman without a lover, because my Piero is never with me!"

A woman with a black mask, long beautiful white hair, and a moss-green smock hobbled toward them with an unusual walking stick – a porcelain walking stick! Fina squinted through her small eyeholes.

"*Dobroho večora*, children," she croaked.

Isa jumped. "My, you are lifelike. Are you a witch?"

"Baba Yaga, from Ukrainian – well, Slavic – folklore. She eats little children like you and lives in a house on chicken legs," she cackled. "And she flies around in a mortar and pestle." She thumped the walking stick, which Fina guessed was the pestle.

"Madam Zora?" laughed Fina. "But it is too marvellous – Ruby and I played a guessing game all day about your costume, but we never considered a witch!"

She put one bony finger to her lips – clearly a rubber glove designed for the occasion. "Shhh! Do not reveal my identity, or I will kidnap you and eat you both!" She hobbled back into the ballroom.

"Spiffing costume—" Fina stopped. Isa had vanished. The hairs on her arm rose as she looked through the glass window in the roof. Lightning. Then great rolling sheets of thunder. A feeling of unreality swept over her as the rain pattered insistently on the roof. The corridor went quiet, all chatter hushed by the rain.

But then she realised it was silent because it was empty and dark.

15

Alarmed, Fina dashed toward the blaring lights and music, but the friendly costumes and masks had become grotesque and distorted. Nothing was different from a few minutes ago, but somehow, everything had changed.

A flash of white light from the windows lit up the room, followed by a clap of thunder.

And then the lights went out.

Instead of expected screams, the room went eerily quiet, as if everyone had frozen in place. Then the whispering started, then a low rumble of chatter.

"*Benvenuti cari ospiti!*" Marchesa Gloria's authoritative voice echoed across the marble parquet. "We have another source of power, but it may take time to fix it. Meanwhile, we'll light the ballroom with candlesticks. Please do not leave my lovely party." She paused. "Besides, you're bound to get soaked!"

Murmurs of laughter and approval came from the crowd. The first candelabra lit up Daria's face. She passed it to a dog-costumed guest and within ten minutes the ballroom glowed in an elegant light. The band members' faces transformed from sullen to delighted. They struck up the eminently appropriate *Mood Indigo*.

A woman in a full-skirted scarlet silk ballgown from the 1700s – Marie-Antoinette – waltzed past with someone in a *Medico della Peste* mask, black cloak, and white gloves. Ruby had told Fina how doctors in 17th century Venice used to wear the long, white-beaked mask while treating the plague. They would fill the beak with plants believed to thwart disease. A symbol of death.

Fina shivered and then smiled as she watched Harlequin and Pixley dancing. She couldn't see Ruby or Iveta, but she guessed Iveta had swept Ruby off to a corner to chat. Or rather, for Iveta to chat while Ruby listened.

"I'll consider it," Marie-Antoinette said to her partner as her skirts brushed Fina's legs. The death doctor rumbled, "But can I count on you?" They twirled away into the crowd.

The elfin-troll expertly guided a goddess toward Fina. For she must be a goddess, given her long, white strapless gown, loose hood, and chains of red beads looping up around the crown of her head. Fina wondered idly whether it was a Zora creation, given its simple, flowing lines.

The elfin-troll stopped, leaned over, and caught his breath. The goddess leaned over and whispered, "Are you ill, Emil? Let me help you upstairs."

"Hazel? Emil?" queried Fina, wide-eyed. "Can I help?"

"*Tcha, nein,*" wheezed Emil. "It is my allergies, *ja*. It creates breathing problems, my asthma."

Fina frowned. What would cause allergies in the dead of winter? Certainly not the cat, as she was nowhere to be seen.

"What caused your allergies?" asked Fina.

Emil's ears flapped as he shook his head. "Sometimes it just happens. Good." He stood up straight and took a deep breath.

"Thank you for your concern. I'm fine now." He turned to Hazel. "Would you like to dance more, *ja?*"

Hazel's hood flapped as she shook her head. "You're an expert dancer, Emil. I'm worn out so I'll hunt down refreshments." She eyed Fina. "Lovely cat costume, Fina, but I thought only men were supposed to wear it."

Fina sighed and explained her love of cats for the umpteenth time. "I can tell you are a goddess, Hazel, but which kind?"

"It seemed an Ethiopian goddess, Atete, would be appropriate. She is the goddess of fertility, though I certainly do not want any children at this time in my life!" She paused, scanning the room. "Speaking of children..." She trailed off as she made a beeline for Sergio and Pixley.

Emil held out a green-rubber hand to Fina. "Care to dance, Gnaga?"

Fina set down her bubbly. "Delighted."

They set off at a rapid pace, as Emil ignored the mellow song. Trickles of sweat rolled down her neck as he twirled her around.

When he finally slowed down for a moment, she asked, "What is your costume, Emil? Is it a troll? Or an elf?"

He gave her a little dry laugh. "Ach, it is Kobold from German folklore. He is, how do you call it? An unclean force."

Fina giggled. "An unclean force? Perhaps I should stop dancing with you now. What on earth is an unclean force?"

"It is a little person who lives in the house and helps with chores. But sometimes he is mischievous and knocks over stools, or hides spoons. If you do not feed him, he becomes angry. But he is good most of the time and likes to sing to children."

"It must be like a brownie or a little person in Ireland. Like the fairies?"

"*Ja,* almost the same. I make sure to leave cream for my

Kobold every night and then my wife, and I have no problems in the home."

From across the ballroom, Fina spied another Gnaga, a large one, twirling toward them. The cat stopped, held out a hand and said, "*Miao, scusi.*"

Startled, Emil jumped back, careening into a nearby Columbina, though this Columbina was not the marchesa. Columbina screeched, either from the personal intrusion of space or because of the alarming creature who had taken it. Emil yelped and caressed Columbina, which only made her curse at him more.

With one swift movement, Gnaga grabbed Fina's arm and pressed her into the dance crowd.

Her Italian stuck in her throat, so Fina said in English, "Thank you for the dance offer, but I'm exhausted – and I must find my friends."

Gnaga gripped her arm tighter, forced the other straight and pulled her close.

"This song is swing, not tango," said Fina desperately.

The large Gnaga was undisturbed by this news, cutting a pathway through the crowd.

The seas parted for them – a field mouse tittered next to the Mad Hatter. Guests had formed lines on either side of them and began to clap. The band's song petered out in a pathetic whimper, save one last crashing of a cymbal.

Fina gulped, suddenly feeling ill. What was that smell? Hair oil?

A wave of revulsion swept over her. The last time she had smelled that odour had been in the cellar. With Vittorio. But that was impossible. He couldn't possibly be back from the dead, could he? Could he have really been visiting his aunt, as Isa had said?

She jerked her arm back. "Let go, you're hurting me!" she hissed. "Everyone's watching and I feel ill." It was true – she was sick from the attention, shock, *and* hair oil.

A deep gurgle of evil laughter came through the smiling cat mask. "Yes, it is I."

Fina's breath caught in her throat. That voice! It had to be him. Every muscle in her body tensed, flooded with fear. But underneath it all was a small spark of relief. She wasn't a murderer after all.

"But I–I–I thought I..." Fina trailed off, scanning the dizzying crowd for Pixley and Ruby, but with her eyes always returning to fixate on the cat's immobile face.

"Shall I tell the police about your proclivity for heavy metal objects? Especially for hitting others?"

"You wouldn't dare. They wouldn't believe you."

"Wouldn't they? You're right, your innocent appearance would make them laugh. But you see, I'm familiar with you and your friends. Involved in quite a few international scrapes with the law? Especially your friend, Mr Marsh. I noticed a poster suggesting I should usher him into police hospitality post-haste."

The room began to spin. "Please, I'll talk to you, but I need fresh air."

"Very well," he said, piloting her to the door. As they crossed the threshold, Pixley waved at her gaily from the corner. He licked a cannoli and laughed at something Harlequin said. Though desperate to signal him somehow, she couldn't even make a face at him with this blasted mask, and Vittorio gripped both her arms.

The corridor's cool air revived her spirits. She could handle this no-good, no-account charlatan. She didn't need Ruby and Pixley for everything. Besides, Vittorio must have had run-ins with the police over his career. He simply oozed 'villain' through every pore.

A few guests loitered at the far end, taking no notice of the two cats.

Vittorio lifted his mask, revealing his all-too-perfect teeth.

"You chose the wrong costume," said Fina in a consciously flippant voice. "You ought to have been a vampire. You know, Vlad the Impaler?"

He threw his head back and cackled, apparently unconcerned the other guests had turned toward them. "I like you very much, dear Miss Aubrey-Havelock. You not only have spirit, but you have fire. A rare quality in English women."

"Would you like to continue your backhanded compliments, or get down to business?" Fina couldn't believe how cool and collected she sounded. The mask helped – he couldn't see her facial expressions, so it somehow emboldened her.

"Aren't you concerned about my well-being? After all, my vanishing act must have puzzled you."

Fina snorted. "You're as mischievous as a fox, Mr Magician. That's what magicians do, don't they?"

"My, my, you're certainly a cooler customer than you were yesterday... and even more attractive." He paused. "But I'm not interested in affairs of the flesh for the moment. No, I'm interested in affairs of the pocketbook. Specifically your pocketbook."

"I haven't a bean. Not a sausage, I'm afraid. And my friends haven't any money, either."

"Come now, don't play coy with me. How else can a university student and her friends gallivant about Europe – and the Caribbean, I hear – without ready cash?"

"We're rather resourceful. And we're invited to fabulous spots, like Lake Como, mostly due to Ruby's formidable design skills. It unlocks many a door."

Vittorio waved a hand dismissively and clicked his tongue. "No matter, then. I thought a little extra dough, as the Americans say, would be the icing on the cake."

"You're mixing metaphors."

"Enough!" he growled. "You will take me seriously, do you understand?"

"Perfectly. Though it's challenging with your getup."

He sighed. "You may play the fool with me all you like, my dear, but the *polizia* may not find your humour quite so entrancing. You and your playmates will smuggle me into England, do you understand?"

"What do you mean, 'smuggle'?"

"Your authorities believe I associate with the criminal classes. I'd be happy to stay in sunny Italy, but alas, one of my associates demands my presence in London."

"How do you propose we smuggle you into the country? In a trunk? There's hardly a trunk that would fit a man of your size. If you're really a magician, surely you can materialise yourself through psychic waves from Como to London."

Ignoring her insult, he replied, "You will not physically hide me, but you will say I am your uncle coming to visit you for a month. I will secure a false passport in the meantime – an easy enough affair to arrange. The authorities will not think twice about a kindly uncle coming to visit a sweet young girl, especially one with an aristocratic name."

"Sorry to burst your bubble again, but as you hinted, the authorities must have me on a list due to my 'activities' – as you call them – around Europe. I'm subject to His Majesty's full scrutiny every time I behold the white cliffs of Dover."

"Well, no matter. Despite the scrutiny, I'm sure you still manage admittance, and that is what concerns me."

Columbina, identifiable as Marchesa Gloria by the pink silk

patch on her gown, popped her head around the doorframe. "Yoohoo! We're about to reveal the costume contest winners – you won't want to miss it."

16

Fina leaned against the wall, staring down at the black-and-white squares rather than the dizzying crowd.

"Feens, are you all right? You're panting like a dog!"

Ruby's face was obscured by the Isis mask.

"It's too complicated to explain now – I'll tell you after the costume contest. Though I am thirsty."

"At your service, madam." Pixley bowed and gave Fina a glass of water, which she downed in one greedy gulp.

"_Posso avere la vostra attenzione, per favore_?" came the voice from stage.

Fina groaned. Il Grande Vittorio was master of ceremonies.

Pixley's glass of champagne slipped through his fingers, tinkling into a thousand pieces. He whispered, "But I recognise the voice – it's Vittorio. Back from the dead."

"Your puns are not appreciated, Pix. Or idioms," hissed Fina. "I had another run-in with the villain."

The band blasted an opening flourish.

"I will announce the winners of tonight's costume contest, and will then perform my best trick."

The lights came back on.

The crowd hooted their pleasure amidst great applause, well-lubricated by free-flowing alcohol. Marchesa Gloria looked up at Vittorio in admiration, while Isa gracefully bounced onto the stage in her Pierrette costume.

"That's not my best trick, but I'll take credit," Vittorio laughed as Daria and Gustavo hurried around with their candle-snuffers, slowly extinguishing the candelabras.

Vittorio cleared his throat. "First prize goes to... Baba Yaga, the Ukrainian witch!"

Zora screeched and cackled, banged her pestle, and then, suddenly remembering her role, hobbled up the stage's side stairs. As this manoeuvre was clearly going to outlast the crowd's short attention span, Vittorio continued. "Next, we have second prize. The winner is... Khonsu, Egyptian God of the Moon!"

Pixley yelped and jumped. He dashed onto the stage. Ruby and Fina yelled, clapped, and stamped their feet. "He's such a ham," laughed Ruby. "Look at him now." Pixley smiled and bowed repeatedly, like a marionette gone awry.

"Third prize goes to the marvellous dragonfly!"

Iveta curtsied, bowed, and fluttered onstage. She bestowed kisses upon the crowd.

Holding out a large hand, Vittorio boomed, "Fourth prize goes to the skeleton that glows!"

Silence blanketed the room. Then tittering broke out, rising in a crescendo.

Behind Vittorio, Marchesa Gloria fluted, "Where is the marvellous skeleton? Has anyone seen the skeleton?"

Everyone spoke, but no one came forward. Fina hesitated, wondering if she ought to say something, but decided against it.

Zora leaned over and whispered to Gloria, who then whispered to Vittorio. He had removed his mask and his face was beetroot red. Was he embarrassed about something? Perhaps he was angry. "Ladies and gentlemen, please give a warm round of final applause for our winners!"

Fulsome claps echoed around the room as Pixley and Zora walked arm-in-arm off the stage.

Isa took the microphone and made a series of rat-a-tat staccato pronouncements in Italian, all too rapid for Fina's addled brain to understand. No matter, it was clearly a list of preliminaries while Vittorio disappeared from the stage. A moment later, he returned in his tight-fitting waistcoat, shirt, and trousers. No cape, no jacket, and no mask. He made a slow twirl with hands raised as Isa narrated. She'd finally slowed down so Fina could understand. "The wonderful Vittorio is unlike other magicians you've seen. They operate with loose capes and flowing clothing – a cheap trick to hide their secrets. Vittorio's clothes cannot conceal anything, as you can see."

Vittorio took the microphone and waved Isa away. "Thank you. That is my dear assistant Isa, who will now help me with my next trick." Isa disappeared behind the band. "Now I need an audience volunteer to prove what you are about to witness is truly magic."

He shielded his eyes with a hand, scanning the crowd. "You! Gnaga! How could I not select a fellow Gnaga for this trick? Please, join me onstage."

Ruby clapped and laughed, oblivious to Fina's sick stomach. Fina shook her head, but the crowd clapped and said in rhythmic time, "Gnaga, Gnaga, Gnaga."

With trembling knees, Fina ascended the stairs. Once again, Vittorio grabbed her arm and piloted her to the side. He clapped. "Please give her a warm round of applause." He gulped down a glass of water as Gustavo and Daria, who had apparently been commandeered for the trick, rolled out a coffin-like box on a large trolley. Isa skipped behind it, and then took Fina's arm.

Narrating, Vittorio said, "Our Gnaga will open the box and knock on it, to make sure nothing is amiss."

Fina glared through her mask at Vittorio. He wasn't seriously going to put her in that box, was he? She'd sooner run away, screaming, all fear of public shaming aside. She was about to protest when Isa whispered, "You're not getting in, silly. You're just proving the box is real." Despite her casual tone, Isa's left hand shook.

Fina sighed and merrily opened the box, peeked in, shook her head and knocked loudly on all sides.

Isa slipped into the box, leaving only her feet and head peeking out.

As Vittorio shut the creaky panels over her, his hand slipped. The crowd gasped at what was obviously a cheap trick. He waved Fina off the stage. She scampered away, glad to be free of the attention and creepy Vittorio.

The guests held their collective breath as Vittorio wielded a large silver saw with teeth resembling his own. He thrust the saw down on the box, causing a great cracking noise.

Fina wasn't the only one to jump.

He chuckled, a man possessed by the rhythmic movement. Only Isa's eyelashes fluttered occasionally – her head was perfectly still.

Fina peered at Il Grande's red face. In addition to the bump on his forehead – her handiwork – a small raw patch on his jaw glowed red from where he had nicked himself shaving. She shuddered. The sawing noise soon became unbearable, though Pixley's hand on her shoulder calmed her slightly.

Was this really part of the trick? Why was it taking so long? As if reading her mind, Ruby leaned over and whispered, "It's taking a terribly long time. Do you think something is wrong?"

The devil near her tittered to the angel. The dog chuckled nervously to a guest in a moon costume.

"Aha!" The saw clanged to the floor as Vittorio pushed apart the two halves.

Blood trickled down the box's inside.

The devil screamed.

And the lights went out.

Again.

17

For once, Fina was the last one to keel over. She heard a loud thump near her, which must have been Ruby. And then Pixley on the other side.

The darkness was so complete she couldn't see anything, and she certainly couldn't hear anything through the echoing shrieks and cries.

The welcome glow of candlesticks turned the inky black to a grey dawn. Gustavo's voice boomed, "*Un momento*. The lights are coming back on soon. *Stai calmo*."

As if Gustavo were a magician himself, the lights switched on again, revealing a chaotic scene resembling a hospital more than a party. Costumed guests were comically strewn about the floor, in various stages of nervous exhaustion or fainting spells. Ruby crouched next to Pixley, gently slapping both cheeks.

"I thought you fainted too!" cried Fina as she crouched down next to Pixley.

Ruby shook her head. "No – I thought it was you!"

Pixley's eyes peeled open and he sat up. "Terribly sorry. I'm normally not squeamish, but the blood, my God, the blood!"

"It was a trick, Pix. No need to worry."

Ruby glanced up at the stage. "Perhaps, but why is Vittorio on the floor?"

The coffin-box lay open and empty, pushed to one side, and Isa was crouching down beside the magician, shaking him. "Grande, Grande, are you ill?" His arm had fallen over his face, so Isa moved it away. "*O mio Dio!*" she cried.

Fina screamed. Il Grande's glassy eyes stared down from the stage at her, made all the more sinister by his impish, dimpled smile.

The scream drew the crowd like bees round a honeypot, creating a humming, buzzing noise. Marchesa Gloria stood over the body, wringing her hands and pacing. Gustavo and Daria approached, only to be repelled by the marchesa's rapid-fire Italian instructions. The *medico* doctor, in his evil-looking mask, bent over the body, making the time-travelling scene complete. He straightened and whispered something into the marchesa's ear.

Pixley hissed, "Who's the chap in the frightening beaked mask?"

"I believe it's Lord Mayhew," said Ruby absently. She stared, unseeing, into Vittorio's fish-like eyes.

"What is it, Ruby? Did you spot something?" asked Fina.

"I remember hearing something ping – like metal hitting the floor – right after the lights went out. There was a moment of silence before the chaos."

Behind her hooded face, Hazel said, "I heard something like that, too. Shall we investigate? It's clear Marchesa Gloria is out of her depth."

And indeed she was. Not only did she pace and continue to wring her hands, but she had become embroiled in a queen bee competition of the highest order. Iveta flapped and fluttered, chattering around the marchesa, while Marie-Antoinette – Marilyn Asher – strode around as if she were back in the lobby of the House of Commons, barking orders at the marchesa. Fina shrugged. At least the three of them were communicating, though apparently past one another.

"Another farrago," sighed Hazel as she sidestepped Emil's flapping ears on her way to the stage.

Ruby was after her like a shot, mirroring Hazel's every step.

Pixley chuckled. "Well, well, looks like Ruby's feeling the competitive heat. A whole new side to our calm and collected friend."

It seemed half the guests were now onstage, milling about and yelling to their friends on the ballroom floor.

"It's complete chaos," said Sergio. "Why is Marchesa Gloria letting this happen?"

"She's completely frozen," said Hazel.

Before Hazel reached the marchesa, Ruby had dashed toward their mutual quarry. Pixley and Fina followed at a leisurely pace. Fina grimaced at the bloodied box, even though the blood was clearly fake. Or at least not human blood. As she averted her eyes, a silver flash caught her attention. She bent down and craned her neck under the box. A silver syringe. Even during the best of times, Fina was squeamish, and she certainly considered needles to be on par with large spiders. Gritting her teeth, she gingerly touched the syringe's tail and lifted it as if she were afraid it would jump out and poke her.

Holding the syringe in front of her, she cut a path toward Ruby, Hazel, and Marchesa Gloria, plus their assembled Greek Chorus of sorts standing behind them.

"*Dios mio!*" cried Iveta.

Emil shrank back. "*Mein Gott.*"

"Good Lord," said the masked plague *medico,* clearly Lord Mayhew.

"Crikey," said Sergio.

Marchesa Gloria's temples throbbed. "Don't this just beat

all." Even in her preoccupation with the syringe, Fina noted the broad New York inflection, and the marchesa's decidedly less-than-regal expression.

Ruby squinted at the syringe, which Fina gladly offered her in Ruby's grandmother's sky-blue handkerchief.

Lady Asher marched toward Marchesa Gloria as if she were sizing up her boxing opponent. "I demand you call the police at once. It's clear this magician was murdered."

"Why do you say that?" asked Hazel.

"She's right," said Ruby, relishing her opportunity to answer Hazel's question. "There's a red flush across his face that was not caused by a heart attack. It's poison, though I must consult a poison book to determine which one."

Hazel's eyes flickered. "Why are you such an expert on poisons? I thought you were a *frock maker*."

Pixley murmured, "Ruby knows her onions."

Ignoring Hazel's mocking tone, Ruby said, "I'm a chemistry student who understand poisons and dyeing processes."

Isa looked up, her eyes red and moist. "Dying processes?"

"She means colour dyes – for clothes," put in Zora.

Lady Asher stamped her foot. "This is all nonsensical chatter. We must call the police, Gloria. Now. If you won't, I will. I won't spend another moment in this house with a madman."

Fina mused that, despite her own tendency to jump to conclusions, Lady Asher took the proverbial cake. Maybe it was appropriate for someone dressed as Marie-Antoinette.

Sergio shook his head. "Marilyn – Lady Asher, you cannot call the police."

"Why ever not? Are they on vacation? Or is Lake Como so crime-free they've decided to dispense with the expense?"

Marchesa Gloria found her voice. "Mussolini has banned all celebrations, and we've violated that rule on a grand scale."

Pixley grinned and whispered to Fina, "How perverse Il Duce's fascist control has led to us being free of the rozzers."

Lady Asher turned on her heel. "What did you say, Mr Marsh?"

Fina marvelled at the woman's hearing.

"Oh, I was just discussing another jolly cockup from Signore Mussolini."

Not to be undone by political circumstances, Lady Asher said, "Well, if we don't call the police, what are we going to do? We have a murder and no way to solve it."

"Perhaps it was one of the outside guests," said Emil.

Gloria shook her head. "I was onstage the whole time, and the only people near enough to get onto the stage were this weekend's guests, or the staff. The band took a break, so they were in the same position as the other guests. And if Vittorio was murdered via syringe, it's not likely someone could propel it from another corner of the ballroom."

Fina surveyed the guests milling about despondently, like children who'd lost their playmates. She scanned the room for the skeleton, but that was the one costumed figure she couldn't find. The devil she'd seen earlier rose and marched toward the stage. He held up his hands and shook them at Marchesa Gloria. Fina caught the words "Let us go" and "now". She realised the devil must have been one of the prominent guests invited from the town, now begging to leave.

Marchesa Gloria nodded and whispered to Gustavo, who turned and tripped over Emil, who fell on Hazel, causing a domino effect cascading across the stage. Lady Asher was the last domino to fall, with a scream.

Lord Mayhew, who lay on the floor like a crab about to scuttle offstage, roared, "Enough!"

The guests froze, as did everyone onstage. Mayhew was the

only one to move, rising and dusting himself off, but not before he threw down his medico mask.

In surprisingly perfect Italian, he said, "You may all leave now as the storm has cleared. Thank you for attending a lovely party with this unfortunate ending. You are to keep quiet about this affair, otherwise there will never be another party in Bellagio."

While Fina was half-irritated by the man's arrogance, she was grateful for the respite from the general hum and chaos. Guests followed Mayhew's instructions readily, murmuring half-hearted goodbyes as they left the ballroom, some still wearing their masks, perhaps in the hope they'd find another party elsewhere.

Mayhew removed his cape, threw it to the floor, and marched toward the crowd around the syringe.

Fina grinned as she caught Ruby scowling at Mayhew. As if reading her mind, Pixley said, "Ready for fireworks?"

Lord Mayhew pointed at the syringe Ruby cradled in her handkerchief. "Let me have a look."

Reluctantly, Ruby held it out.

"No, I mean, let me have it."

"Why? Are you the police?"

"Don't play with me, girl, give me the syringe."

"My name is Ruby, not 'girl'. And I'm not giving you the syringe until you tell me your qualifications. I'm certain mine are more advanced than yours."

Once again, Mayhew took on an odd colouring, signalling imminent apoplexy.

Iveta intervened. "Really, Lord Payhew..."

"It's Mayhew!"

"So sorry," fluted Iveta. "Ruby, darling, has such experience with murder, that I'm sure we're all happy to let her solve the mystery."

Ruby gave Iveta a wan smile – the smile of someone who is half-infuriated, half-grateful for a friend's well-meaning intervention.

Marchesa Gloria cleared her throat. "I am the one in charge here. And from what I know of Ruby and her friends," she gestured toward Pixley, and then wavered as she looked at Fina, "we need their help to solve this mystery. You will all give them your full cooperation."

A mutinous murmur broke out among the guests. Marchesa Gloria held up a finger. "Stop your grumbling. We must solve this murder, and we must solve it quickly. I'm afraid Lord Mayhew's warning to our guests will scarcely keep tongues from wagging all over Bellagio tomorrow. It's only a matter of time before the local police or Il Duce's thugs show up at our door. We must have answers for them when they arrive."

Ruby cleared her throat. "Thank you, Marchesa. Pixley, Fina, and I will ask you all brief questions tonight, with more to follow tomorrow, as it's late. I suggest you all retire to the dining room while we set up for questioning in the library."

Marilyn Asher sniffed and waved her Marie-Antoinette handkerchief, channelling her character rather than her own personality. "It's much too late, and we've all had too much to drink. Questions shall be asked tomorrow," she said, as if they were readying themselves for Prime Minister's Question Time.

The marchesa shot a venomous look at Marilyn, who returned her steady gaze. "Dear Lady Asher, if we do not begin tonight, not only will memories disappear, but the police will appear. Though we've asked guests to keep quiet, it's possible they'll show up tomorrow."

Ruby bestowed her most dazzling smile on Lady Asher. "Would you prefer to be questioned by them?"

18

Despite grumbling guests' continued protests, they all filed into the dining room, leaving Ruby, Fina, and Pixley to the library.

It was a relief to be ensconced somewhere cosy and warm. Fina scanned the walls of ancient books appreciatively. She ran her finger along the spines, noticing layers of dust covering these sadly unloved, unread volumes.

"Feens? Are you there?" Pixley's nose peeked over the high-backed chair he pushed toward the centre of the room.

"Sorry – my mind is spinning. When that happens, it shuts down and I go into a trance."

Ruby snapped her fingers playfully. "Well, it's time to return – I asked Gustavo to make espresso. Now, I want both of you to tell me everything you know about the guests' families."

Fina had learned not to ask why Ruby needed such information, so she and Pixley told her everything they'd heard since the beginning of their journey, starting with how she'd chatted to Sergio by the ferry dock. While they talked, they arranged three high-backed chairs in front of the glowing fireplace embers. Pixley poked the charred log and consulted his watch. "I'd better build up this fire if we'll be here much longer. I spotted a few snowflakes when I was on the terrace."

"When did you go on the terrace?" asked Fina.

"A few times, ah, for a bit of fresh air."

"Don't let him fool you, Feens. He was canoodling with Harlequin."

Though Fina expected fulsome protests, a tiny smile played across Pixley's face.

A gentle tap came at the door.

"Must be Gustavo." Fina padded across a thick rug.

But a tear-stained Pierrette stood there, made even more pathetic by the painted tears rolling down her cheek.

"Come in, come in." Fina grabbed Isa's hand and piloted her to the seat facing Pixley and Ruby.

Isa blew her nose, producing a duck-like honk. She crumpled into the seat, creating an odd, rag-doll effect.

The warm security of the velvet upholstered chair seemed to reassure her, and she perked up enough to say, "I had to speak to you before the others poisoned your mind."

Interesting choice of words, thought Fina.

Pixley pushed his spectacles up the bridge of his nose and leaned forward. Fina half expected his nose to quiver. "Do tell."

"Something wasn't right when we started the trick."

"How so?" asked Ruby.

Isa twisted her handkerchief. "Everything went wrong – not dramatically, but with little things. I dropped the vial containing pig's blood."

Ruby nodded. "Which would explain why the hem of your frock is tinged with blood."

Fina stared. Selkies and kelpies, there *was* blood on Isa's frock! She shook her head, disappointed that her normally observant self hadn't seen it.

Isa shuddered. "Yes. And Vittorio dropped his handkerchief. He never drops anything – at least not intentionally."

"Mmmm..." murmured Pixley. Ruby and Fina stared at him. He looked up from his notebook and said, "I meant, 'mmm' because I imagine magicians are not in the habit of dropping things. They must be extremely coordinated."

"Precisely." Isa nodded. "Despite his size, he was graceful and exact in every movement. Dropping the vial didn't bother me, but as soon as he dropped the handkerchief, I had a premonition something would go dreadfully wrong."

Ruby tapped her teeth. "Tell me. Do you recognise this syringe, or know why it was onstage?"

"I've never seen it and I avoid needles at all costs. I do not like them."

Gustavo slipped in and set down a tray of espressos with biscuits. Fina pounced, sighing with relief. Her stomach had been in so many knots she hadn't eaten – for once.

"We did not find a mark on the body, though we haven't made a thorough check yet." Ruby sipped her espresso. "Did you see anything before or after the lights went out that might give us a clue?"

Isa shook her head and stared at the biscuits. Pixley offered her the plate. "Would you like one?"

"Ah, no, thank you. I was thinking, remembering. The only other peculiarity was Vittorio himself. His face was as red as a pepper – as we say in Italian – even though it wasn't too warm onstage."

"I noticed he was red as a beetroot," said Fina. "I thought he might not feel well."

"It would explain why he dropped things," said Ruby. "Red as a beetroot..." She trailed off.

Isa nodded. "He must have been unwell, though he was healthy all day."

"Did his aunt recover?" asked Fina.

"His aunt?" Isa blinked. "Oh, his aunt. Yes, it turned out she had a, what do you call it – when your stomach grows large?" She motioned to her own stomach, trying unsuccessfully to make it grow large.

Pixley tapped his pen on his knee. "A bilious attack."

"Bill-ee-us?" Isa looked at them as if English were an unbelievably stupid language.

"How long have you worked for Vittorio?" asked Pixley.

"I met him when he visited Predappio – my hometown near Bologna. I had trained as a gymnast, and Vittorio was searching for an assistant. He said he'd visited many small towns to find a gymnast he'd train as a contortionist. My family was poor and he offered me money and the chance to travel. That was two years ago, and I've been happy since then."

"Why were you invited this weekend?" asked Fina.

Isa's ringlets quivered. "Vittorio said he'd received an invitation from the marchesa, along with two tickets for travel to the villa. We were travelling to Paris via Venice, so it made perfect sense to stop for a few days here."

"Do you have any idea why she invited you two?" asked Ruby. "Beyond providing a performance?"

"Vittorio said we were performing at a masked ball."

The trio exchanged glances but said nothing.

Isa rose. "If you haven't further questions, I'll retire. I'm exhausted."

"I can well imagine," said Ruby. "I have one more question."

"Yes?"

"Why did you lie to us?"

19

Isa twisted her handkerchief so tightly it turned her finger a ghastly white. "What–whatever do you mean? Lie?"

"You said Vittorio visited his aunt, which is why he vanished. But that story is preposterous – it's daft as a brush."

"Daft as—?" Isa's heavily lined eyelids rose.

Pixley set down his espresso. "She means it's a poor explanation. Do tell us what really happened. Vittorio is dead so it cannot matter."

Her slight body plopped back down into the chair. "You're correct. He doesn't even have an aunt – at least not one who's alive. I, too, thought it was 'daft' as you say, but I had no reason to push him further on it."

"What did you think he was doing?" asked Fina.

Isa let out a little cough. "I believed he was having an assignation – an affair, I believe you call it."

"An affair with someone elsewhere? Or with someone here?"

She shrugged. "Vittorio travels so much, he has women in many cities."

Pixley clicked his tongue. Fina grinned at Pixley's decidedly inconsistent Victorian personality.

Ruby pressed further. "But was his lover here, in Bellagio – or even at the villa – or somewhere else?"

Furrowing her brow, Isa said, "I couldn't say, because he was secretive about it. But I had the impression he stayed near the villa, but not exactly in it. Maybe he took a room in Bellagio."

"Why did you have that impression?"

"It's silly, really, but he didn't pack enough warm clothes to go too far."

"Were either of you acquainted with any of the other guests before you arrived?"

"Vittorio knew Zora because they ran in the same aristocratic circles. And the marchesa, of course."

Shimmering green-and-blue wings fluttered in the doorway. Iveta.

Much better to invite her in than leave her eavesdropping, thought Fina.

"Iveta, please come in," said Ruby before Fina could open her mouth.

Like the *Queen Mary* gliding into port, Iveta entered. Isa frowned. "What is she doing here?"

"Darlings, I have a frightful headache – most likely from the cheap *prosecco* Marchesa Gloria served – so I'd like to be questioned next." She looked down at Isa, as if she were an unfortunate choice of furniture.

Glowering at Iveta as she rose, Isa tramped to the door, trailing her bloodstained hem behind her.

Pixley rose and fussed about with the interrogation chair, as if he could make it more comfortable.

"Pixley, *carinho*, please do not trouble yourself. I shall stand, as I may fall asleep if I sit down." Iveta leaned against the chair, as if it were one of the many men Fina had seen her with during their Lisbon travels.

Pixley sat down. "Please tell us what you remember of this evening, Miss Da Silva."

Iveta's eyes twinkled. "So formal, Mr Hayford. I'm so sorry – you're Mr Marsh now."

Ruby, Fina, and Pixley glanced at each other, but Iveta saved them from having to explain.

"No need to explain, dear Pixley, I change my name sometimes when I feel like someone else. Life is much more exciting that way, especially when one is caught up with many, how do you say – stuffed people?"

Ruby smiled. "Stuffy people."

"Ah, you always understand me, Ruby, my gem." Her small, delicate hands flew to her face. "But this evening! What a disaster."

Fina nodded. "Death is always disturbing."

"I did not mean Vittorio's death, *carinho* – that kind of man will always have a shortened life – but the party! Terrible champagne, a bandleader with no sense of timing, and the marchesa... but the costumes were delightful, as was the food, despite the lack of it."

Pixley cleared his throat. "Yes, I'm sure we all agree with you, but would you tell us what you observed?"

Iveta squeezed her eyes shut. Her suddenly flat voice made her sound like a medium telling their fortune. "I remember Vittorio disappeared for a while. I danced with many people. I saw a skeleton who made me shiver—"

Though reluctant to draw Iveta out of her trance, Fina intervened. "You spied the skeleton as well?"

Her eyelids flew open. "But yes. So eerie and... like death haunting the room." Iveta's fluting tones had returned, and she now sounded like a voice actress on the wireless. "I only noticed the skeleton once, in the corridor. After it turned and waved to me, it disappeared."

Pixley cleared his throat. "And you won the contest."

"Only third prize, darling."

"Did you notice anything unusual when you went up onstage?"

"You mean like a syringe? No." She paused. "But Vittorio was so red – and thirsty – poor dear. And the little contortionist was sweating. And the marchesa looked upset." She flung out her hands. "I only notice people, my darlings, not things around me. Though I do love some precious things, such as jewellery." Iveta gazed lovingly at her robin's-egg-sized emerald ring.

"Why would someone kill Vittorio?" asked Fina, growing weary of Iveta's perpetual good cheer.

Iveta levelled a piercing stare at Fina. "Didn't you know? He is a magician in all senses of the word. He is a swindler, a con artist."

Fina was unaccountably relieved her conversation with Vittorio hadn't been a figment of her imagination.

Pixley licked his lips. "Do tell. All the details." His pen hung over the paper, ready for any rapid-fire words.

"A marchesa had her jewellery stolen at a weekend party a year ago. I was there, and I'm certain it was Vittorio or his assistant who had sticky fingers, not the marchesa's maid."

"Were you able to prove it?" asked Ruby.

"No, but I saw him coming out of her room – what other reason could there be?"

Ruby and Fina exchanged a look.

"While she was elsewhere," Iveta said pointedly.

"Anything else?" asked Pixley.

"A friend told me he disappeared from another house party after a similar incident."

"Why did you call him a swindler? Isn't he just a thief?" asked Fina.

"Ah, my little one, you are alert! I cannot prove it, but

Vittorio performs tricks often involving someone's jewellery –
from an audience volunteer. Because he spends time at these
houses, I believe he has replicas made of particular rings, neck-
laces, and earrings. Then he deliberately selects the lady
wearing them, makes them disappear and then reappear—"

"But the reappearing version is a fake," said Ruby.

Iveta nodded. "I cannot prove it, but in my line of work, I've
come across several surprising discoveries. Ladies often want to
sell their jewellery to me, discreetly, away from their husbands. I
am invited to appraise jewellery and often to buy it myself and
provide a replica. In the past six months, I've told no less than
three women their precious stones were already paste, much to
their genuine surprise. The one thing they all have in common
is Vittorio's visit."

"Did you go to the police?" asked Fina.

Iveta's half-mast lids indicated she was rethinking her
appraisal of Fina's intelligence. "No, *carinho*, of course not. In my
line of work, one avoids the police. Not that I ever do anything
illegal, of course, but because discretion is my business, I cannot
afford to become entangled with those ruffians."

"So you do not have any proof," sighed Pixley.

A whining scream like a scalded cat crept through the
doorway.

20

The wails continued as they all dashed toward the dining room. As she careened around the corner, Fina slipped on the polished parquet, her ankle going out from under her. Gustavo caught her as she crumpled to the floor. He held her tightly, lifting her onto a nearby bench.

His hooded eyes scanned her face. "Are you injured, miss?"

Fina rubbed her ankle. "Thank you, Gustavo, but it's probably a momentary twist. You know how it is when your ankle gives out."

He blinked.

"You wouldn't understand, I suppose, unless you wore heels." She paused. "Would you help me toward the dining room? We must find the source of that dreadful scream."

He held out his arm at an angle. "*Naturalmente.*"

The pair turned the corner into the dimly lit dining room. Soft white flakes brushed against the windowpanes, lightening the darkness outside. Despite herself, Fina gasped with pleasure at seeing the snow, a true rarity in the lowlands of Lake Como.

Candlelit shadows fell across guests' faces, creating obscured half-masked countenances. But no one lay on the floor or looked injured. Sergio held a cigarette languidly to his lips, a Harlequin contemplating his lost Columbina. Hazel sat next to him, methodically turning a fork repeatedly, her face almost entirely hidden by her hood. Zora paced in front of the window, as if Baba Yaga had been grounded from flying in her mortar and pestle. Emil, who still wore his droopy house-spirit ears, stared at his own feet. Lord Mayhew drummed his fingers portentously next to his evil doctor's mask on the table. Lady Asher's lips puckered in disapproval – at what, Fina did not know. Daria, the maid, held a dustpan and brush, but she made no move to sweep up. Instead, she slid a figurine across the mantel, then another next to it, in an almost compulsive neatening gesture. Isa relaxed in an armchair by the fire, a faint smile playing across her lips. Perhaps she was relieved to have finished her questioning.

Ruby turned her own half-hidden face toward Fina and Gustavo. "Fortunately, everyone is fine. The marchesa and Daria screamed because they spied the infamous skeleton at the window."

Fina gulped. "You mean he's still out there? I had begun to think he was just a merry prankster from town."

"That grin," moaned the marchesa. "So frightening against the darkness and glow of the snow."

"Did he knock on the window? Or seem to want anything?" asked Ruby.

Daria sniffed. "He waved and then disappeared."

"Selkies and kelpies," said Pixley underneath his breath.

"Pardon?" asked Emil. "I am not familiar with this English phrase."

Fina waved him aside. "It's a made-up phrase – no need to learn it."

Lady Asher cleared her throat and stood up. "This nonsense must stop. I'm going to retire."

For a moment, Fina thought she meant she planned to retire from Parliament, and then realised she meant go to bed. Fina herself longed to be under the covers, even in that horrid room. Maybe the cat would warm her feet.

The marchesa looked at Ruby. "We're nervy and exhausted. Could we finish the questioning in the morning?"

Again, it struck Fina as odd the marchesa was so willing to lend the reins of power to a stranger. But perhaps she recognised she was out of her depth.

Ruby leaned over and whispered in Pixley's ear. Fina wasn't near enough to eavesdrop. Pixley smiled and tore sheets of paper from his notebook. He whispered to Daria, who nodded and disappeared.

"We're all fatigued and upset, so I suggest you spend a few minutes writing what happened. I'll give you three questions to answer – you may write in Italian if it's more comfortable." Ruby turned to Lord Mayhew. "While we're waiting for Daria, I wonder if you might lend me one or two of your heart pills."

He spluttered, "Whatever for? I need these pills."

"I just need one or two. *Please*. We must eliminate the possibility the pills are connected to Vittorio's death."

Lord Mayhew wriggled his jaw from side to side and then handed her a few pills from his box. "Don't know what you expect to find, but fortunately I brought more than enough."

Daria reappeared, with a fistful of pencils. She handed one to each guest, who now also had slips of paper from Pixley.

"Here are the three questions." Ruby had honed her authoritative 'I'm in control' voice over the course of their eight murder cases together. Fina remembered how the first time she had used it, Ruby's voice had been steady and confident, but did not have the bold, honey-like texture it did now.

"Question one. Who invited you to this weekend party and why?

"Question two. What was your relationship with the deceased?

"Question three. Who are you?"

FINA SHUT her bedroom door and wrinkled her nose. What was that odour? Must be dry rot. Or mildew. She sighed as she looked down at bedclothes dating to Roman times. Just as she pulled back the covers, something moved. Two somethings moved. Two large black dots came into focus. Spiders!

She yelped and jumped back. Recovering her wits, or at least half of them, she grabbed her sponge bag and nightgown and marched out of the room. Her fright had turned to anger, suddenly erasing all semblance of cautious movement or behaviour. The corridor was dark. And quiet. Someone wheezed in the room opposite. A galloping noise rushed past her and then she spotted two yellow eyes. It was the cat, whom she had named Puffy since no one had bothered to introduce them. At least some creature was enjoying themselves.

Her fingers brushed against the smooth wall, a door, and then a wall again. As she was debating whether the next door was Ruby's, she heard Hazel's voice. "They'll never guess, Sergio, and we've been terribly careful."

Footsteps came nearer the door. Fina sank back into a recess in the wall.

"What if the police show up tomorrow? Then we're well and truly sunk."

"How would the Italian police know what happens in London? Besides, I'm sure they're country bumpkins who will barely speak any English."

Fina stopped breathing as the door opened and a figure tramped out. By the heaviness of the step, she surmised it was

Sergio. Once he closed the door to his room, Fina continued her journey, deciding she'd finally found the right door.

She tapped on it lightly. Footsteps approached and the door opened a crack. Ruby smiled and held open the door.

"Well, well, look what the cat dragged in," chuckled Pixley. "Are you seeking refuge in Ruby's room or are you anxious to discuss the case?"

"A bit of both, actually. There are spiders in my room."

Both Pixley and Ruby shuddered and nodded. No further explanation was needed.

As Ruby poured tea from an enormous pot, Fina contemplated telling them about the conversation she'd overheard. Pixley would be upset Sergio was seeing Hazel, and Ruby would be upset because... would she be upset if her rival was in another relationship – clearly not in one with Ian?

"Here's your tea, Feens. Are you there?" Ruby held out a cup of steaming milky tea.

Fina wrapped her hands around the cup. "Sorry – I was lost in thought."

"Please take us with you if you have a flash of inspiration about the murder." Pixley sat with his legs crossed, surveying the room. "I haven't decided if your room is better than mine, dear Ruby. Yours is a tad bigger."

"I am here to work for the marchesa, while you, Mr Marsh, are a mere secretary," she chuckled. Her smile dropped to a frown. "I hate to break up our tea party, but I've just remembered what we need to do."

Pixley groaned. "I have a sinking feeling it involves leaving this cosy room."

Ruby nodded as she slipped into a scarlet dressing gown. "We need to examine the body once more – without everyone else's prying eyes."

Fina shuddered. "How about you two go and I'll watch over the room? Someone may try to harm you again, Ruby."

"Oh no you don't," laughed Pixley. "Besides, how are you going to fend them off if they have a weapon? No, if someone wants to hurt her, it's better we're all together and out of the room. If they want to try again, we'll all be here, ready to pounce together."

"Are you sleeping here?" asked Fina.

Pixley punched an orange velvet pillow on his chair. "But of course. I'll sleep upright here, even though I'm hesitant to besmirch Ruby's reputation by sleeping in a lady's room."

"Enough banter, dear ones. Let's slip downstairs before the murderer takes action."

ONE LONELY SPOTLIGHT lit the ballroom stage. Darkness blanketed the room, save the glowing snow brightening the French windows. Floorboards creaked as they took the stage, despite their best efforts to slink along like cats.

Underneath the white sheet normally used for the grand piano lay Vittorio's body, creating a monstrous white blob.

Pixley held up a finger. "What was that?"

"What?" hissed Fina.

"Sounded like cutlery clanging."

A plate and cutlery crashed. The trio froze, though Fina's eyes scanned the ballroom. "Hello?" she croaked.

No answer.

She heard a rapid pitter-patter.

Pixley held a hand to his red jumper. "It's the blasted cat."

"It's not a blasted cat," pouted Fina.

"Children, we must focus." Ruby sat on her haunches and lifted the sheet. She mumbled what sounded like a children's rhyme under her breath: "Hot as a hare, blind as a bat, dry as a bone, red as a beetroot and mad as a hatter."

"Pardon?" said Pixley.

Ruby shook her head. "I knew something wasn't right about the way he died. Remember what Isa said in her interview?" She took out a pair of small silver scissors and snipped away under the sheet.

Fina grimaced. "What are you doing?"

Ruby ignored her, finished her task and snatched Vittorio's face mask. "Let's hurry to the kitchen. I must conduct a few experiments on Lord Mayhew's pills and these materials."

For once, they had made the correct footwear decision – stockinged feet. Fina hurried behind Ruby and Pixley, slipping and sliding every time her feet hit the marble floor in between the plush rugs. Her ankle ached where she'd turned it earlier that evening. As they turned down the low-ceilinged stairway to the kitchen, it gave out again with a stab of pain, sending her careening toward a large hall table. She grabbed it with both hands, jolting the telephone off its cradle. As she scooped up the receiver, she heard a crackling noise. Gingerly, she put it to her ear and waved away the impatient Ruby and Pixley. She mouthed, "I'll join you."

Crackle. Silence. Breathing. As she listened, Fina slowly turned round like a lighthouse, taking in her gloomy surroundings. Nothing stirred, other than the telephone receiver. She covered her own mouth, worried whoever was on the other line might hear her breathing. Memories of the villa flashed before her, room to room. Fina's photographic memory revealed telephones in the library, another outside the ballroom, and at least one upstairs, near the bedrooms.

The breathing continued, so loudly Fina had to suppress a giggle. Then it stopped as the phone clicked. A faint breathing joined the heavier breathing. A muffled voice said, "*Gattara.*"

The line went dead. Certain one voice must be on the upstairs telephone, Fina dashed upward, pulling herself up by the banister as she went. When she arrived at the landing, her muscles tensed. What had she been playing at? Now she was alone in a dark corridor with someone who was a likely killer. She froze and then inched her way into a corner near the landing. From this vantage point, she could poke her head out like a turtle to survey the scene. There was a light further down the hall: a spotlight from a torch being waved around. Fina shrank back, confident she couldn't be spotted, at least not from the bedroom corridor. Her head poked round the corner. The torch provided just enough light for Fina to spy a figure moving toward a bedroom door. Then her knees nearly gave out from under her again.

The figure pushed on Fina's bedroom door.

21

Fina's eyes fixed on her bedroom doorway, even though the figure had disappeared inside. A minute later, it emerged, slowly shutting the door.

Light footsteps pattered up the stairway. Fina swung round in terror and dashed across the corridor to a broom cupboard. The door stuck, so she pulled and pulled, trying not to grunt.

The footsteps were very near.

The cupboard door flew open, sending an army of brooms cascading to the floor with a terrific crash.

"Feens!" hissed Pixley.

Fina grasped her chest, panting. The footsteps were Ruby's and Pixley's.

The sound of bedroom doors swinging open and crashing shut filled the hallway.

"What the devil?"

"*Meu Deus!*"

"*Bozhemiy!*"

Lord Mayhew, Madam Zora, and Iveta came into view, dressed in impeccable dressing-gowns. Lord Mayhew wore a silk navy smoking jacket, Madam Zora a stiff high-necked black-

and-white affair, and Iveta a foamy emerald chiffon number with high-heeled slippers.

Other heads popped into the corridor, as if it were an advent calendar opened all at once by an overenthusiastic child. Pixley cleared his throat and stepped forward. "We're dreadfully sorry for the commotion, everyone. We needed to conduct a thorough search – everything except the bedrooms. The broom cupboard was apparently overfull, so that's what caused the kerfuffle."

Lord Mayhew crossed his arms. "What were you searching for in the broom cupboard?"

"Brooms!" blurted Fina.

Ruby and Pixley stared at Fina.

"I mean, it's all part of the investigation, but I'm afraid I'm not at liberty to discuss it at the moment."

Mayhew threw up his arms and opened his mouth, as if to continue. But it snapped shut as soon as Madam Zora and Iveta spun on their heels. The consummate politician, Mayhew could not perorate without an audience. He frowned, mumbled, and followed in Zora and Iveta's footsteps.

Pixley clapped his hands together silently. "Well done, Feens. A simple, yet brilliant strategy."

Ruby shook her head and opened the door to her room.

"Wait," hissed Fina. "Come into my room for a moment."

Ruby grimaced. "It's disgusting in there, Feens. Must we?"

"We must!"

Once inside, Pixley and Ruby stood near one another, well away from the wall or furniture.

Fina chuckled. "You won't catch the plague in here." She perched on the bed and scanned her surroundings. "I spotted someone enter my room, just as you two came up the stairs. I thought you were someone else – perhaps the murderer – so I tried to hide in the broom closet. Chaos ensued and I lost track of the mysterious figure."

"Was your door unlocked?" asked Ruby.

"Yes, I didn't see any reason to lock it. I noticed it was ajar. But nothing's been disturbed."

Pixley blew on his spectacles and wiped them. "The miscreant might not have had enough time."

"But what does Fina have that would interest anyone?" asked Ruby.

"Are you implying I'm not interesting?"

Ruby opened her mouth but Pixley beat her to it. "Whatever has come over you, Feens? You're feisty, as usual, but never like this with Ruby."

Fina blew out her cheeks. "I haven't a clue. Maybe it's this room. Sometimes I feel like I play second fiddle to Ruby, and this room was that personified."

"Symbolised, you mean," said Pixley.

"Don't push her, Pix." Ruby put an arm on Fina's shoulder. "You're right, Feens. I can't help how others treat you, but I shouldn't ever take you for granted. I'm sorry. Will you forgive me?"

Fina crossed her arms and stuck out her bottom lip. "Of course I will." She paused. "But it's infuriating how perfect you are sometimes. Just now, you offered the perfect apology. You took responsibility and apologised, full stop."

Pixley giggled. "You can't blame her for giving you exactly what you wanted. Besides, we're all het up after the past few days. I'm not perfect like Ruby, but I'm perfectly knackered."

"Assuming the person was after something in Fina's possession, what could she have that someone would want?"

"Nothing. Absolutely nothing," sighed Fina. "And it's not as if I have anything that could incriminate the murderer."

Ruby shivered. "That means they wanted to harm you."

FINA WIGGLED her nose and inhaled as the smell of fresh bread wafted to her pillow. She blinked at the bright light streaming through a crack in the drapes. Pixley sat directly in her line of sight, his head back and mouth open slightly. He snored like a bleating lamb.

She jumped. Ruby was bent over in the corner, fixing something. It was only Ruby, Fina thought. Her nerves had been shot to pieces and she couldn't shake a nagging feeling that their old nemesis, Moriarty, was nearby. Moriarty had followed them from England to their subsequent adventure in Lisbon, hounding them but never truly injuring any of them.

"Rise and shine, lazybones!" cried Ruby.

Pixley's head snapped up and back with an abrupt snort. "Where am I?" He rubbed his neck. "Now I remember – I slept in this blasted chair in your room, dear Ruby."

"And I'm sure Fina and I are grateful for your generous protection," smiled Ruby.

"And your snoring," mumbled Fina.

"I didn't hear you, Miss Aubrey-Havelock." Pixley wiped his spectacles, placed them on his nose and peered expectantly at her.

Fina drifted back to sleep. A skeleton offered her flowers, while a group of masks danced around them. She heard a voice say, "Only coffee or tea will revive her. Fortunately, Gustavo prepared us a generous lunch with coffee."

Fina bolted upright. "Coffee? Yes, please."

Pixley and Ruby laughed as Ruby handed her an espresso.

"Did you say lunch?" Pixley consulted his watch. "Selkies and kelpies, it's one o'clock! What time did you get up, Ruby?"

"At eleven. I've been busy in the kitchen. They let me have a quiet corner to conduct some more experiments. I didn't have enough time last night to confirm my suspicions for certain. I let you two sleep – we didn't get to bed until almost five in the morning." She munched on a slice of toast. "I asked Gustavo to prepare all our favourite foods and to make sure we wouldn't be disturbed. But they'll expect us sooner rather than later – or at least the marchesa will want our report."

"What report?" Fina sank her teeth into a large piece of toast drizzled with olive oil.

"The one revealing the murderer."

"How on earth could we do that? We haven't reviewed their statements. And I don't know what you two found after your experiments in the kitchen," said Fina.

Pixley rose. "You tell her, dear heart, while I freshen up in the bathroom."

"I knew something wasn't right when we were on stage after he died, but I didn't really start to put it together until Isa said 'red as a pepper' and then you said 'red as a beetroot'."

"Didn't you mumble something about it – like a children's rhyme – when we returned to the stage last night?"

Ruby nodded. "Hot as a hare, blind as a bat, dry as a bone, red as a beetroot and mad as a hatter."

Fina blinked.

"It's a saying to remember what happens when someone dies of atropine – better known as belladonna – poisoning. Vittorio was very red, his fingers fumbled closing the box on Isa, and he was also thirsty. Even if it had been due to the warmth, why wasn't he sweating like Isa?"

"Even if that were true," said Fina, "why wouldn't the syringe still be the cause of death? Why test Lord Mayhew's pills – and why on earth did you snip Vittorio's clothes and take his mask?"

"At first, it was just intuition that the syringe might not be the cause of death." Ruby spread marmalade on a small square of toast.

Fina swallowed. "Why?"

"It seemed too theatrical. If I were the murderer, I'd use a syringe because it would go untraced. The whole point of injection is to make it seem like a heart attack or another sudden illness. But if you wanted it to look like a heart attack, why leave the syringe on the stage?"

"I wondered about that. At least there's one point in my favour," sighed Fina.

"Then, once I questioned the syringe, and thought about the symptoms of atropine poisoning, it became obvious. First of all, I tested the syringe and found there was atropine in it, as we might expect if the murderer wanted to throw suspicion on it. That would limit the suspects potentially, to those close enough to inject Vittorio, and those who had access to a syringe."

"But why not just make it seem like a heart attack? Why bother with the syringe at all?"

Ruby tapped her teeth. "That's been bothering me, too. The only plausible explanation is that they realised I was a chemical expert – and an amateur detective – after someone tried to poison me. I have no doubt the information spread like wildfire after Iveta got hold of it. The murderer knew about the distinctive atropine flush, which would not appear in a heart attack victim, and figured they'd better throw suspicion on others."

"I'm still puzzled as to what put you on to the fact the syringe wasn't the murder weapon."

"It's so simple, you'll groan when you hear it."

Fina groaned.

"Spiffing," Ruby laughed. "The atropine symptoms occurred *before* he could have been injected. To add to that, there's no way he could have somehow been injected in the dark and died instantaneously. Atropine isn't like cyanide. It does take a bit of time."

"I think I understand. You're saying that at the very least, someone would have had to inject him well in advance – and he'd have definitely been upset or said something about a masked individual poking him with a needle."

"Exactly. So Lord Mayhew's pills seemed plausible, but when I tested them they turned up negative. That didn't necessarily eliminate him or his pills from suspicion, however, as he could have given me non-poison pills. We'd only have his word for it."

"So this murder was not only planned, it was planned well in advance," said Fina.

"It seems so."

"And yet I keep coming back to that syringe. What was it doing there, on the stage? Do you suppose it could have been part of the plan that went wrong?"

"There's an idea," said Ruby thoughtfully. "But to return to our findings in the kitchen, Pixley and I discovered his clothing was not poisoned."

Fina's espresso cup clattered in its saucer. "Poisoned clothing? Wasn't that a myth concocted by detective story authors?"

Ruby shook her head. "It's rare, but it's possible. Of course, it helps if the victim has a cut that rubs against the poisoned clothing. But that's neither here nor there, because the poison wasn't in the clothing."

"But what does that leave?" Fina squinted with the effort of remembering last night's scene in detail. "It can't have been the water he drank, because he was already showing symptoms by that time. And no one had access to his equipment." The scene played out in her memory, unspooling like a film. "Wait – Ruby, you took his mask, too! So... the mask was poisoned?" gasped Fina.

"Yes, I tested it yesterday. The criminal in this case gets top marks for ingenuity."

"Explain the mechanics. I cannot understand how a poison mask kills someone."

"There are a few ways it could happen." Ruby held up the

mask with a handkerchief and shuddered. "As this is a full-face mask, Vittorio might have ingested small amounts of poison through the mouth opening. It could have also crept in through the tear ducts or skin. That would speed up the process. Vittorio was obsessive about shaving, too, and I noticed a tiny nick on his jaw, probably made the day of the murder or the previous day. It would certainly be the best route for the poison."

"But how could the murderer depend on him cutting himself?"

"They couldn't. Which means it's possible he did it the day before, and our murderer saw their opportunity to take action. Either that, or they depended on other methods of ingestion."

Pixley emerged from the bathroom and rifled through the suspect statements. "It seems convenient and risky at the same time. Our murderer took a lot of chances."

Ruby frowned. "That's what troubles me. The crime was planned so precisely, and yet it was sloppy. Higgledy-piggledy."

"That's not all that should be troubling you," sighed Pixley.

Ruby and Fina looked away from the mask.

"Madam Zora's and Lady Asher's statements are missing."

22

Ruby squawked, a decidedly un-Ruby-like squawk.

Pixley created a neat square of sheets on the bed, leaving a hole in the corner. "See? They're gone. Someone must have pilfered them last night, while we were downstairs."

"It could've been the figure in my room," said Fina. "Perhaps they stopped at Ruby's room first – I wouldn't have seen them since I was still walking up the stairs."

Ruby rubbed her forehead and dropped into a nearby chair. "What does it all mean? My brain is still in a fog from that awful acid attack."

Fina smiled. "Your brain in a fog is like most people's brains on a clear day. You found the real murder weapon, not the syringe."

"Thank you, but we should let people continue to think it was the syringe, not the mask."

Pixley pulled down his red jumper. Fina wondered if he would wear it every day for the rest of his life. Probably.

He cleared his throat. "Let's review the other statements before any other disaster occurs, such as fires, floods, or a plague of locusts."

Ruby ran a finger over one sheet. "Let's begin with Hazel Padmore."

Fina snuck a glance at Pixley. The corner of his mouth lifted ever so slightly.

"Hazel Dido Padmore. Lives in Ladbroke Grove, London. Question one. Who invited you to this weekend party and why? She says Marchesa Gloria invited her to write her memoirs a month ago. Hazel says the pay and prestige led her to agree, though she says she and the marchesa miscommunicated."

"That's true," said Fina. "Pixley and I overheard the conversation – Marchesa Gloria thought Hazel could churn out her memoir in a weekend."

Pixley snorted. "Only a non-writer would say such a thing. Hazel said she was here only to gather material, an eminently reasonable plan."

A flash of irritation spread across Ruby's face at the implied compliment.

Pixley lit a cigarette. "But what seems unreasonable, or rather inexplicable, is why she was at the Ethiopia negotiations."

"Hasn't she worked with Emperor Selassie?" asked Fina.

"Yes." Pixley exhaled a long stream of smoke. "But she's not here in any official capacity."

Ruby smiled. "Would you ask your boyfriend, Sergio?"

"He's not my boyfriend," said Pixley, a little too vehemently. "But I will ask."

Ruby continued. "Question two. What was your relationship with the deceased? Answer: Never met him before, but saw posters for his performance in London." Ruby tapped her teeth. "Now we arrive at my favourite question. Question three. Who are you? Hazel says she's vice-chair of the International African Friends of Abyssinia and secretary to the deposed empress. She says she's here to do whatever is necessary to free Ethiopia."

Fina swung a crossed leg. "Her statement rings true since she's obviously a serious and dedicated person." Her leg swung harder. Should she tell them about her eavesdropping on Hazel and Sergio?

"Fina Aubrey-Havelock. The rate at which your leg is swinging indicates you're hiding something," said Pixley.

"Do tell, Feens."

Fina shrugged. "It's true. Why did I even try? But you must believe I thought I was protecting you."

The only response was a stream of smoke directed upward from Pixley's mouth.

"Last night, as I walked to Ruby's room, I overheard voices – Hazel and Sergio."

Ruby and Pixley leaned forward.

"Hazel said something about no one guessing because they had been so careful. Sergio asked what they'd do if the police appeared tomorrow – meaning today – because they'd be 'sunk'. Hazel said the Italian police had no idea what went on in London, so they'd be safe."

Pixley let out a low whistle. "Well, well. Sergio and Hazel. And we also saw Hazel with Emil in the church."

"She's a hussy," growled Ruby.

Pixley munched on a biscuit. "Ruby Dove! I'm surprised. You're jealous?"

"She has a point, Pix," said Fina. "Hazel with Sergio, Emil, and possibly Ian."

"I'm surprised at you two, calling yourself modern women," laughed Pixley. "Just because a woman has a relationship with a man does not mean she's intimate with him. I mean, look at your relationship with me!"

"Speaking of relationships, let's read about Sergio." Fina snatched the paper before Pixley could grab it. "Sergio Chapman. Lives in Cambridge, not surprisingly. Question one. Who invited you to this weekend party and why? Answer: Marchesa Gloria. He says he was invited for the negotiations."

Fina stared, blinking, at the empty food tray. "He's lying. I don't know why, but he's lying. On the ferry crossing, I asked him who invited him and he said it wasn't Marchesa Gloria, but a friend of a friend."

Ruby glanced at Pixley. "You never told us how you came to be Mr Marsh."

Sighing, Pixley plopped into a chair and ran his hand over his bald pate. "A mutual friend, a journalist, set us up together."

"Did they ever," giggled Ruby.

"Touché, Ruby, darling. I hadn't met Sergio before coming here, but we both knew I was a journalist posing as his secretary."

"Why did he agree to it?" asked Fina.

"I haven't a clue, except he's keen to kick the Italians – and the British, should they try anything – out of Ethiopia. It must have seemed a natural thing to invite a sympathetic journalist. Besides, I've proved to be an able assistant."

Fina couldn't help herself. "You certainly have, *Mr Marsh.*" She smiled and continued. "Question two. What was your relationship with the deceased? Answer: None. Never seen or heard of him before this weekend. Question three. Who are you? I'm a British top-secret agent..."

Ruby and Pixley gasped.

"Just joshing!" moaned Fina. "I mean, that's what he wrote. Then he said he's a Cambridge law professor."

"Why did you ask question three, Ruby?" asked Pixley.

"I asked that to make guests less guarded when answering question one. That's what I really wanted to discover."

"But surely the murderer wouldn't give you the correct answer just because you asked," said Fina.

Ruby tapped her teeth. "Questions one and two can be verified and checked out, correct? For example, we've already caught Mr Chapman in a lie, which means he may be telling more lies—"

"Or he's lying for another reason," put in Pixley hastily.

"Correct. But the point is not so much to gain information, but to find out who was lying."

Someone thumped on the door. Fina stiffened. That was not the polite tap of the marchesa, nor the discreet knock of Gustavo.

A gruff voice boomed in the corridor. "*Polizia*. Open, please."

23

The trio froze, staring at one another. Pixley flew into action, grabbing fistfuls of paper. Fina followed, crumpling sheets and stuffing them under the bed.

Ruby fluted, "Who is it? I'm dressing."

"*Polizia.* Open, please."

Fabulous, thought Fina. What an imaginative police force.

Kicking the last sheet under the bed, Pixley nodded at Ruby. She opened the door.

A flurry of black uniforms, followed by the rolling gait of Italian commands, filled the room. Fina and Pixley stood still, hands behind their backs. The smell of shoe polish, hair oil, and leather was so overpowering, Fina fell back into a nearby chair.

A tall man in a dark grey suit loped into the room, as if he were returning home after a long day at the office. He puffed on a cigarette, tapping the ash into a small metal box. Then he lifted his head, revealing a craggy yet appealing face behind his brown trilby. He smiled and nodded at Fina, Ruby, and Pixley, before placing his overcoat and hat on a hook near the door. "Please leave," he said in Italian to the sentries. The creak of shoe leather was all Fina heard as five officers filed out.

"Please forgive my men," said the man. "They can become a little, ah, *overentusiastico* sometimes." He held out a hand to Ruby. "Commissario Giudici, at your service."

Ruby shook his hand, smoothed her skirt, and sat on the bed. She waved in Fina's direction. "These are my friends, Miss Fina Aubrey-Havelock and Mr—"

Pixley coughed and stepped forward. "Mr Pixley Marsh."

Giudici's thin mouth turned up into a crooked half-smile, rather like a child's drawing. "Pleased to meet you, Miss Aubrey-Havelock and Mr... Marsh."

Pixley stood with his hands behind his back, making forward rolling motions on the balls of his feet. Fina had never seen the normally calm Pixley so nervous. Ruby shot her a worried look from across the room.

Giudici scratched his head. "You seem familiar, Mr Marsh. Have you travelled to Bellagio before?"

Fina gulped. She scanned the room for a distraction she could throw the commissario's way. After dismissing falling over the used crockery near the door, she did the next best thing.

She let out a heavy sigh and crumpled to the floor, trying to fall on the rug, not the hard floor.

"Fina!" cried Pixley and Ruby.

Fina heard a general commotion, then felt herself being lifted and placed on the bed.

"Here, put her feet up on this box," said Giudici. "My aunt has fainting spells, so I'm accustomed to helping. We need odour salts."

Fina nearly let a giggle escape her lips.

"I believe you mean smelling salts, Commissario," said Ruby.

"I'll find them!" said Pixley in a strained, high voice. A door slammed.

Fina's eyes nearly fluttered open at the next sound she heard. Singing.

Giudici's gentle lilting voice sang in Italian, something about little boats on the sea.

"Um, that was pleasant," said Ruby.

"I sing a children's lullaby to my Zia when she faints. It almost always brings her back, even before the—"

"Smelling salts."

"*Vero.*"

Though Giudici's aftershave smell was light and pleasant, it was mixed with the heaviness of tobacco – more than enough to revive Fina's sensitive nose. Perhaps she should open her eyes before he wondered why Pixley had vanished.

She batted her eyes like a film star and cried, "Where am I?"

Fina detected the smallest eye-roll she'd ever seen on Ruby's face.

"You had a fainting spell, Miss Aubrey-Havelock. Now you've awoken like a marchesa in a dream," said Giudici.

Now it was Fina's turn to blink. What a peculiar policeman. Maybe he was an aspiring poet or writer.

"I heard a song – was it my dream?"

"Commissario Giudici was singing," said Ruby in a flat voice.

Giudici smiled and threw his hand up as if he would sing an aria, which, in fact, he did. This time, his voice was deep and loud, but the performance lasted only a minute. His hand-waving caused his tall but slim frame to slide off the silky bedcover onto the floor.

Fina gaped at Ruby. She held a hand over her mouth, smiling. Was he drunk?

His hand appeared, grasping a piece of paper. Then his head popped up with that crooked smile on his face. "Madam Zora Misko. Born in Lviv, Ukraine. She was invited by the marchesa to revamp her wardrobe, though she says Marchesa Gloria's tastes run counter to her own. Question two—"

"I can explain, Commissario," Ruby interjected.

He held up one forefinger and continued. "Question two: What was your relationship with the deceased? Response: an acquaintance."

Well, that was a lie. Hmph. An acquaintance.

"Question three." Giudici looked up. "Fascinating questions. I will finish. Question three. Who are you? Response: a world-famous designer of clothing for the daring and adventurous."

Giudici planted a fist on the bedspread and lifted himself up. "Would you explain why these fascinating questions are underneath your bed, Miss Dove? I wonder what else might be under there – perhaps the murderer? Or perhaps the four contest winners from last night?"

Ruby's furrowed brow cleared as she stared past Giudici. "I'd be happy to discuss, Commissario, but I think we'd better leave the villa. Now."

Fina followed Ruby's line of sight.

The sunny day had become overcast, obscured by billowing puffs of grey smoke.

SCAMPERING AND SCUFFLING noises followed cries of "Fire!"

Giudici dashed through the door, still grasping Madam Zora's questions.

Fina's arms tensed, then her legs. Her heart beat fast and her mouth turned to cotton wool as the smell of smoke wafted through the now-open window.

As she ran to the door, a hand stopped her. Ruby whispered, "Slow down. This is a centuries-old stone villa and we have hordes of police who will take care of it. Besides, we need to talk."

"But we still need to leave. Now!"

"Yes, but let's take our time." She threw on her coat.

Fina took a deep breath and counted to three – a new technique her doctor had prescribed for her so-called nerves. Her arms and legs relaxed, though her heart still beat fast. She slipped into her coat and followed Ruby. But Ruby stopped in the doorway. "Wait. Ought we to collect those sheets before Giudici returns?"

"No. I'm sure he saw others, and he can simply ask the other guests if they also answered our questions. Then we'll be caught in a lie – it already looks like we're hiding something."

"You're right." Ruby's heels clacked across the marble floor. "But what shall we do about Pixley? He gave Giudici his false name, and it won't take long for him to discover his real identity."

"And that's not all," sighed Fina. "Pixley's brother is wanted by the police."

Ruby halted. "Pixley has a brother?"

"It's incredible, isn't it? Though I don't wonder he's never mentioned him." As Fina retold the story to Ruby, she bumped into Daria, who was running full steam ahead toward the kitchen. Her white cap flew onto the floor.

"*Scusi.* So sorry, Miss Aubrey-Havelock."

"No, it was just an accident." Fina scooped up the cap and was about to hand it to Daria when she stopped. Inside was a piece of newsprint, pinned to the corner. Before she peered at it, Daria snatched it and planted it firmly on her blonde updo. Without another word, she continued her jog.

"Peculiar," murmured Fina as they stepped into the lounge overlooking the smoky terrace. "Did you see what she had in her cap? I couldn't read it."

"It is odd indeed." Ruby opened the French doors onto a chaotic scene. It wouldn't have been chaotic had it not been for a young officer flapping his arms about.

Fina whispered to Gustavo, "What is he doing?"

Without cracking a smile, Gustavo intoned, "He is imitating a chicken."

Cheeky, thought Fina.

Gustavo coughed and continued. "My apologies. I mean, he is explaining what he did when he discovered the terrace conflagration."

Ruby leaned in. "It appears a heap of dead leaves was set alight. Why all the commotion?"

"No one knows how it began, and the young officer is upset he did not witness the arsonist in action. More upset, I'd say, than the commissario."

Giudici lit a cigarette, and then put both hands on the officer's shoulders like a straitjacket. It did the trick, restoring the terrace to its usual winter silence. As Giudici puffed on his cigarette, his eyes narrowed, crinkling at the corners. He stared at Ruby and Fina, but then stepped past them, indoors.

"Should we follow him?" whispered Fina to Ruby.

Emil's small head popped up between their shoulders. "Follow who?"

"The commissario," said Ruby, smoothing her hair. "He was interviewing us, so we were debating if he wanted us to continue."

"*Tchja*, I expect he's looking for Herr Marsh."

Fina and Ruby exchanged glances. "Why do you say that, Emil?" asked Fina.

"Because Herr Marsh started the fire. I saw it with my own two eyes."

24

Crouching behind a juniper bush, Pixley suppressed a sneeze. Blast it. He felt a cold coming on. As he pulled his handkerchief from his pocket, a woollen cap fell onto the muddy ground. *Just what I need*, he thought as he pulled it on over his bald pate. *Much better*, though in the grand scheme of things, this was hardly progress.

"Commissario! Commissario! *Fuoco!*" called a young police officer as he scampered indoors.

Splendid.

Pixley turned his head to the left, right, and behind him. Walls everywhere, walls covered in dead vines. If he could climb over, he'd dash into town and wire London for confirmation of his identity. Or perhaps a local library would have one of his news articles. After all, several had been translated and published in the Italian papers.

The same young police officer returned, doused the fire with two jugs of water, and retreated inside. Giudici, Ruby, and Fina milled about on the terrace. Ruby, who never slouched, stood like an officer ready for inspection, while Fina's shoulders drooped. She looked defeated. Giudici stepped inside, leaving

Pixley with a strong urge to call out their names. But he spied the young officer pacing just inside the door. He was about to make a run for it, aiming for a small opening in the wall by the villa's perimeter, but then reconsidered. If Ruby or Fina spotted him, they would surely call his name.

And then he saw Fina remove her shoes and Ruby slip them into her pocket.

What were they up to now?

Pixley scrunched his eyes shut as Ruby lifted Fina onto a ledge. His eyelids opened once he realised their backs were to him. This was his chance.

His feet sank into the wet, sweet-smelling earth as he half-crawled, half-ran toward the opening. Finally standing up fully once he reached the wall, he paused to catch his breath. Then he froze again.

Voices drifted toward him from the terrace.

"I recognised he was a criminal the first moment I saw him," said Daria, spitting out the words in Italian.

"How?" It was Gustavo.

"His eyes. His shifty little eyes!"

"Come now, Daria. You must have another reason."

"Besides the fact of his colour, I saw a poster in town. With his face. And he was burning paper in his room. I found the scraps and told the police."

Pixley's heart pounded so hard, he was afraid it would burst and ruin his beautiful red jumper.

"Well, well. We'd better cooperate with the police this time. But only this time. A perfect way to distract them, no?"

RUBY PACED in little circles around the green handwoven rug in the library. The crackling fire tried to cheer her up, to no avail.

A cough broke the silence. It came from a high-backed chair facing the window.

Ruby changed her pacing direction toward the window and soon found Lady Asher with a book on her lap. The black lettering read *The A.B.C. Murders*, but the book was not being read. In fact, Marilyn Asher's head had lolled to the side. Her perfectly made-up face and neatly pressed navy wool frock looked fresh, as if she were not, in fact, asleep in a chair.

Ruby moved a hand close to Lady Asher's shoulder. She snapped it back. Should she wake her? But she'd coughed, so she must not be in a deep sleep. It was deuced peculiar.

As this was not a time to observe social niceties, Ruby touched her shoulder. "Lady Asher, are you awake?"

"Mmmh?" Her eyes flew open and stared, in that unnerving way cats do when they're observing you from afar.

"I'm sorry to wake you, but I wanted to be sure you're feeling fine. After recent events..."

"Quite right, child, quite right you are." Lady Asher smoothed her skirt and touched the corners of her mouth, checking whether her lipstick had slipped. "I'm accustomed to long nights – with politics, you develop the stamina of an ox – but I'm unusually exhausted from last night's events."

"It's probably the shock," said Ruby, in a world-weary way. She doubled back as she realised Lady Asher might be affronted by her tone. "But I'm sure you familiar with that as you're in politics."

Lady Asher sniffed. "Are you implying I'm regularly embroiled in scandal, young woman?"

"Well, I—"

"Because if you're referring to the Frobisher affair, then you're sadly mistaken."

"Frobisher affair... that was last year, was it?"

"Two years ago, probably when you were still in short

trousers. Or a short frock." She waved her hand dismissively. "The point is, the court cleared me of any involvement."

Ruby's mind whirled. "But wasn't Lord Frobisher indicted? I thought you two were close." Frobisher was the only MP she could remember who might travel in Lady Asher's social circles.

With an uncharacteristic snort, Lady Asher replied, "Frobisher was an unmitigated, loathsome bounder. He promised me campaign assistance in exchange for supporting his harebrained schemes in Brazil. Like the generous fool I am, I went along with it." She thumped her heel. "No more. Never. Do you hear me?"

Ruby drew back. She had clearly struck a nerve.

The clock ticked while Lady Asher stared at her nails.

The welcome sound of footsteps fell across the threshold.

"Ruby, darling!" Iveta floated in on a cloud of red chiffon, her gown's plunging neckline softened by a yellow scarf tied at her neck. "What are you doing with this dreary woman?"

Lady Asher rose and marched to the window without another word.

Throwing her usual caution to the wind, Ruby said, "We were just discussing Brazil, Iveta."

"The best country in the world, of course."

A catlike smile crept across Lady Asher's profile. "Then why do you spend all your time in Europe, Miss Da Silva?"

Iveta shooed her away and made a 'pfffttt' sound.

"Are there iron mines in Brazil, Iveta?" asked Ruby.

Iveta shrugged. "But of course, my precious gem. They're not as exciting as the jewel mines, of course. There are—"

"And are you familiar with the Frobisher affair?"

Iveta's gaze, which up until now had been flitting about the room like a hungry songbird, now focused on Ruby. "Yes. Why do you ask?"

"Lady Asher was involved in that scandal. Did you know?"

Lady Asher clicked her tongue and turned toward the window.

"Ah!" cried Iveta. "I knew it. I also knew you had a devious streak, my little Ruby. Maybe we can..."

Ruby held up a hand. "The scandal, Iveta? Tell me about it."

"Well, I was staying with friends in Cairo at the time, but a friend brought a few Rio newspapers for me, dear heart. I devoured them, as there was little else to do. It seems Lord Fishcake—"

"Frobisher," came Lady Asher's voice, unable to let the mistake go.

Iveta smiled. "As I said, Lord Fishcake invested in an iron mine in the interior. There was a series of dreadful accidents and everyone who invested lost their money."

"But why was it a political scandal?"

"Lord Fishcake used his MP position to make promises he couldn't keep. He also somehow involved a few government ministers, so the government ended up footing much of the bill for the mine."

Lady Asher's hands shook.

"You foreigner, you vulgar hussy..."

Iveta bounced up, and pushed up a red chiffon sleeve. "You wish to fight?"

Ruby, already positioned between the two women, rose to her feet.

"Dear Ruby, do not try to stop me. Ever since that weekend in Wiltshire, that woman has been nothing but trouble," said Iveta.

"Ahem," came a voice from the doorway.

Commissario Giudici grinned at Ruby.

"Miss Dove, Lady Asher, and Miss Da Silva. I must ask you a few questions. Would you please join me in the kitchen?"

25

Pixley lit a candle and prayed. Prayed to the god he did not believe in, hoping he'd make an exception for an unbeliever. Maybe an Italian god was more merciful. Perhaps not, he thought as he remembered Ethiopia. But that was the government.

He shook his head as his thoughts looped around. He must focus, and the church was the best place to do so. Nodding at the same old woman he'd met yesterday, he sat in a pew in front of a large pillar, hoping it would make him invisible should the police appear.

Reading often calmed his restless journalist mind, so he picked up the nearest Bible and let it fall open. John 6:1. It was in Latin, but Pixley recognised the loaves and fishes story from his schooldays.

Loaves... his stomach rumbled. Delicious Italian bread with chunks of cheese would make his stomach content, but his brain still worried.

Fishes... fish... fishing. In the dead of winter, no one would be fishing, would they? But fishermen must have little sheds near the water. Yes. He remembered seeing a few places used to store fishing gear in winter – though obviously not on the wealthy side of the lake. No one would search for him there.

Pixley was so thrilled with his new plan that he let the Bible slide to the floor, creating a great cracking sound.

Voices echoed down the nave.

"YOU SEEM to have misplaced your shoes, Miss Aubrey-Havelock. And would you tell me what you're doing here?" Giudici sat on a nearby chair, humming.

Fina lowered herself on the bed, trying to gain more time to consider her answer. Ought she to tell Giudici about the newspaper clippings? Though she wanted to, she knew she'd better consult with Ruby first.

"Shall I give you more time to ponder your answer?" he said, pulling out her shoes from his overcoat pockets. "I had your friends empty their pockets after we discovered something interesting in the kitchen."

"Oh? What was that?"

"The remnants of an experiment. The cook made a fuss this morning about her kitchen being invaded. I had a feeling your friend – Miss Dove – was involved. So I asked her and her two friends to accompany me to the kitchen."

"But why did you search them?"

"I couldn't help but notice Miss Dove's pockets were bulging. I wanted to be fair, however, so I asked Lady Asher, Miss Da Silva, and Miss Dove to empty their pockets. Imagine my surprise when I found these shoes. I assumed they didn't belong to Mr Marsh, so I deduced, like the detective I am, it was you."

Fina brushed her damp fringe to the side and sighed. "Before I tell you my story, Commissario, I must hear yours. What did you find in the kitchen?" She knew well what he'd found in the kitchen – Ruby's chemistry experiment – but she wondered if Ruby had told him the truth.

"Miss Dove said she'd been carrying out a chemistry experiment on Vittorio's clothing and mask."

"Did she, now? And what did she find?"

Giudici flicked a bit of ash from his cigarette. "You know that very well, Miss Aubrey-Havelock. She found poison on the mask."

A long stream of air fluffed her fringe. At least she had one less lie to keep straight. "Yes, I'm sure Ruby told you she didn't think the syringe killed him. So she needed to experiment on his clothing and mask."

Giudici's wide brown eyes bored into Fina's as if he were consuming her. "We also found those answer sheets in Miss Dove's bedroom. I'm puzzled as to why you three believed you could keep that secret, since everyone completed one."

Fina shrugged. "We haven't had many positive experiences with the police, Commissario." She paused. "Present company excluded, of course." She smiled.

"Buttering, oiling – no, flattery will get you everywhere." He smiled back. "But now we arrive at the real question. Why have you been traipsing about without your shoes? And why did Miss Dove carry them?" Then he held up a hand and shut his eyes as if averting a scandalous scene. "If this is a private matter between the two of you—"

Giggling, Fina replied, "No, Commissario." She took a deep breath. Pixley was already in hot water. Better make a clean breast of it, particularly as she had no idea where Pixley was hiding. "Ruby and I believe Pixley started the fire in the garden as a distraction."

He blew a smoke ring. "*Vero*. Absolutely."

"You knew?"

Giudici leaned forward. "Miss Aubrey-Havelock. Whatever

your impressions of the police might be, I assure you our local force are not blithering idiots. What's more, I do my best to ensure my men are well trained because we do not want any interference."

Fina blinked. "Interference? You mean from the *carabinieri* and Mussolini's henchmen?"

Giudici leaned back, his eyes ranging over Fina as if he were reassessing her. "No comment. The point is, Mr Marsh – or whatever his name is – fled the scene. Now, I do not believe he murdered Vittorio, but he is fleeing the police for a reason. You must share that reason with me."

The door flew open, making Fina jump. Then she relaxed. It was Ruby. Fina leaped up and led her to a nearby chair, as if she couldn't see in front of her face.

"Ah, Miss Dove. I told you to remain in your room."

Ruby bit her lip and smiled in her best contrite manner. "I couldn't sit in there alone, wondering what had happened to both my friends!" A well-timed tear rolled down her face.

Giudici stared and then smiled. "Well, now you're here, I suppose we can clarify a few things with Miss Aubrey-Havelock. Though I'm in no hurry."

Fina stared at Ruby and said slowly, "We were discussing why Pixley fled. Would you like to tell him or shall I?"

Giudici put one long finger against the side of his face, listening intently.

With an almost imperceptible nod, Ruby said, "Pixley Hayford, for that's his real name—"

"Why is he travelling under a false name? Is it because he is wanted by the police?"

Ruby and Fina glanced at one another. Ruby held up her chin, defiantly. "Pixley Hayford is an internationally acclaimed journalist. You can confirm it by searching old newspapers."

"Moretti is already doing that."

The hairs on Fina's arms stood on end. She had underestimated Giudici.

"Yes, well, as a journalist, and one interested in the Italy-Ethiopia war, he wanted to report on secret negotiations."

He nodded as if this were all old news.

"You already knew this?" Fina's mouth hung open.

"I'm afraid the marchesa has an irresistible need to gossip. She told us everything about the negotiations. But please go on, Miss Dove."

"He posed as a secretary to Mr Chapman. In a completely unrelated incident, however, he discovered his face on a police poster."

Giudici hummed and then stopped. "And now I suppose you'll tell me he's not a criminal?"

"That's why I lost my shoes, Commissario." Fina gulped. "Let me start at the beginning. Pixley has a brother – I didn't know he had a brother until a few days ago – who is a thief. The brother hasn't spoken to Pixley in ages. They resemble each other, which is why it looks like Pixley is on that poster. But it's not Pixley. I climbed into his room to find the newspaper clippings to prove his identity. Ruby held my shoes for me and lifted me up to the balcony, which is why I look a fright."

Ruby motioned to her forehead, making a wiping gesture.

Horrified, Fina rubbed her own forehead, revealing a great deal of dirt.

He smiled. "You look *bellissima* to me, Miss Aubrey-Havelock, but yes, it does seem you've been playing in the mud."

As Fina felt her face turn hot, she diverted attention by pulling the clippings from her frock.

"Will these clippings prove his innocence, Commissario?" asked Ruby.

As he sorted through them, he frowned. "I'm afraid not, Miss Dove. There aren't any photographs, so whether it's Mr Marsh or Mr Hayford, it doesn't matter. What matters is Pixley looks like the poster of his brother, if it is indeed his brother and not just him."

Fina put her face in her hands. She hadn't even contemplated the possibility that the truth wouldn't be enough for the police.

"Why don't we ask Hazel Padmore or Sergio Chapman?" said Ruby quietly.

Giudici slapped his knees. "By all means, if you believe it will clear this up. But you must remember, Miss Dove, I'm here to solve a murder, so I must continue my inquiries."

Ruby blinked. "But I thought you suspected Pixley of the murder – that's why you were so interested in him."

Giudici shook his head. "I'm not ashamed to say I am a gut-policeman."

Fina looked up. "Gut-policeman? Oh, you mean you're intuitive."

"Intuitive! Yes. The other police frown on me, but it works. But only if I do not eat a large meal," he said, going into his buffoonish act again. "The police are looking for your friend, but in connection with other crimes, not this one. No, I must focus on this crime, which is why I need your assistance."

"Our assistance?" Ruby and Fina said in unison.

"*Assolutamente.* I've heard about you from my colleague in Lisboa, Comissário Cardoso. He is a much more straightforward policeman, but I respect him. He said you helped him on the case."

Fina fought an urge to say that was scarcely the way it had been at the beginning.

A knock came at the door and young Moretti's head popped in.

26

"Commissario, the marchesa wants to speak to you now. She's discovered something important."

Giudici clicked his tongue. "What has she discovered, Moretti? One mystery is more than enough for me."

"I do not know, sir. She says it's urgent and you should meet her in the Occult Room."

"What is the Occult Room?"

Moretti shrugged. "I will show you."

Rising to leave, Giudici said, "I hope you'll both join me in the Occult Room, though I cannot compel you to do so." Without waiting for their reply, he loped away, patting Moretti on the back as they went.

Ruby rushed to the door, slammed it shut and leaned against it. "Thank goodness we can talk for a moment."

"I thought he'd never leave, the way he kept smiling at me."

"I believe our commissario is as sweet as honey on you, dear Fina."

Ignoring the implication, Fina said, "Sweet? I've never heard you call a police officer sweet."

"Well, it fits in this case, doesn't it? We must take him up on his offer to assist him."

"Why? Can't we sit out a murder case for once? Besides, we must find Pixley!"

Ruby twisted her opal pinprick earrings and sighed. "You're right about finding Pix, but not about the case. Have you forgotten your little... shall we say, involvement, with Vittorio?"

Fina's stomach clenched – she had suppressed the memory. Or was it repressed? What would Dr Freud say? "You're right, but isn't that less of a reason to be involved? Surely it has nothing to do with the murder. They were separate incidents."

"But how will it appear to an outsider? You cosh him on the head, he disappears, reappears without warning, and is then murdered?"

"Mmmm... especially if anyone finds out about our conversation when he tried to force me to smuggle him into London." Ruby's wide eyes reminded Fina she had not shared that tidbit with her, so she retold the story.

Ruby stamped her foot. "I have it. I'll assist Giudici while you search for Pixley."

"But you'll have all the fun – and will stay warm while you're doing it!" pouted Fina.

"Dearest," said Ruby, holding out her hands. "If you stay, you'll reveal something – involuntarily, of course – about your involvement. And your Italian is much better than mine, not to mention you'll blend in more."

"With red hair?"

"You know what I mean."

Fina sighed. "You're right. But before I go, let's ask Hazel and Sergio if they can confirm Pixley's identity. Perhaps it will count for something?"

"Excellent idea, Feens. Let's find that hussy."

"Ruby Dove!"

Once Fina had put on at least three jumpers underneath her long herringbone coat, they knocked on Hazel's door.

"Who is it?"

"It's Fina."

Hazel flung open the door, as if she had been standing right next to it. Her jaw clenched as she spied Ruby standing behind Fina. "Yes, what is it? I'm busy with the marchesa's memoirs."

Hazel's desk was perfectly bare, save a small typewriter. Busy indeed.

"So sorry to disturb you, but we had a question – it's urgent." Fina took a step forward, but Hazel held the door half-closed.

"I say, have I missed the party?" Sergio was ambling down the corridor with his hands in his pockets, jangling loose change.

"Sergio! Splendid," said Ruby.

His face broke into an impish grin. "Right. I mean, well done."

"Alright, Sergio, don't get overexcited," said Hazel. "These ladies were just leaving, weren't you?"

Ruby pushed forward past Fina. "I suggest you change your tone, Miss Padmore. Fina and I have been seconded to the investigation."

"Good show," said Sergio.

Hazel glared at him. "Oh, and what gives you the right to barge into my room?"

Fina said, "We must confirm Pixley's identity. You can confirm he's a journalist, correct?"

"I've never met him before this weekend," said Hazel blandly. "And as for a Mr Pixley Marsh newspaper article, I haven't seen one."

"But his name is Mr Hayford, actually," said Sergio.

"I'm not familiar with a Pixley Hayford, either," said Hazel.

"But surely, given your involvement in pan-African circles with Ian Clavering, you must have—"

Hazel crossed her arms. "No, I'm sorry, Miss Dove. You're mistaken. I've never heard of your journalist friend."

They turned to Sergio, who had a streak of sweat running down one cheek. It certainly wasn't a tear. "It's true Pixley told me his real name was Hayford, but I couldn't swear he was indeed Pixley Hayford. He could have just told me that's who he was."

Ruby marched down the corridor without looking back.

STANDING by the shore of the lake, Pixley whistled a soft tune and let his arms flap gently, with his hands in his pockets. His studied nonchalance wouldn't fool Ruby or Fina, but it could certainly do for the locals, he thought as he nodded at a bespectacled grey-haired woman peering at him from a balcony.

Cheer up, old chap, he told himself. The day is sunny, you're in Italy... and what? You're about to hauled off to jail for your brother's crimes? The gently lapping waves distracted him from these unprofitable thoughts. Near the empty lakeshore stood a row of brightly coloured sheds – or were they shacks? No matter, the sun hit a soft orange shed, beckoning him like a jack-o'-lantern.

With a quick twist of his head, he confirmed he was alone, save the vociferous gulls fighting over a delectable lake morsel. The dock creaked and groaned like an unoiled door to a musty attic. He pushed against the door to his glorious orange cottage. Nothing. It was just a cutout door, so there was no handle or lock. Then he tried the next door, this time to a sky-blue shed. He took a running leap and threw himself against the door, busting it open as he tumbled onto the floor. Crawling on his knees, he peeked round the corner to ensure no one had come running. Only a lonely shore crab looked at him, and then scuttled away.

Pulling himself up, Pixley brushed down his trousers and his lovely red jumper, exposed by his open overcoat. Sucking in fresh air, he surveyed the shed's interior. It appeared fishermen used these sheds as storage rooms and as cottages, perhaps for when they planned to go out early in the morning. A long narrow bed stood flush against one wall, while a small rickety table stood against another. In the corner, he spied a makeshift kitchen with a plate, cup, utensils, and a lantern-like stove with a box of matches. The tiny cupboard below the counter held cured meats, a jar of herring, and another jar of unidentifiable vegetables. Next to that stood a large, lidded jug of water.

He smiled at the tiny painting of a whale on the wall and lit the lantern. The flame flickered to light, casting a warm glow inside the shed. Pixley sat down on the bed, and listened to the waves.

His eyelids drooped, calmed by the mesmerising rhythm. As he began to drift away, still sitting upright, he heard a whisper.

"Pixley. Pix..."

27

Giudici struck a match against his shoe. "Where's your friend, Miss Dove?"

Ruby bit her lip. "She had business in town. Women's business, you understand."

The match fell from his hands, but he caught it just in time. "*Ahi!*" He waved his hand as if to cool it down. "I see. Well, I'm delighted you've joined us."

She surveyed the Occult Room, shifting in her seat uncomfortably. Unlike the villa's other rooms, this one had blood-red walls, lined with purple, star-covered velvet drapes. Colourful jars stood next to books with titles like *Stregheria* and *Everyday Spells* in English. Bric-a-brac stood on a nearby table, lit by a green candle. Presumably it was an altar. A white skull stared at Ruby balefully from the mantel. She shuddered.

Giudici pursed his lips and nodded his head, also surveying the eclectic surroundings. "*Stregheria.* It means 'witchcraft' in Italian."

She stared again at the skull. Giudici followed her line of sight and leapt up. "Here, let me." He turned the skull's face toward the wall.

Ruby sighed. "Thank you. That's much better, though this room makes me uncomfortable."

He smiled back at her, his eyes unblinking. "*Precisamente.* That's why I've chosen it." Then he leaned down and pulled up a folder from underneath his chair. "The statements you so helpfully took last night." He thumbed through them and handed them to Ruby. "Who shall we start with, Miss Dove?"

Ruby flipped idly though the papers, not reading them. In the spirit of the Occult Room, she closed her eyes and pulled out one sheet. "Marchesa."

Giudici nodded. Though he remained motionless, a faint sound caught Ruby's ear. A scratching noise. Like tiny claws on wood. She squinted into the darkest corner and caught a flicker of movement, making her jump. When her eyes adjusted, she saw it was Moretti, who had been taking notes in the background the entire time. He rose and left the room.

"Young Moretti is impressively silent."

"The man's like a cat." Giudici sucked on his cigarette. "We locals are fond of the marchesa. She arrived here about ten years ago, and proceeded to consistently invite the locals to parties." He cleared his throat and winked. "Though those parties are strictly forbidden, you understand."

"What do you know about her? She sent me a letter requesting I design a gown for this masked ball event. She's obviously American, but that's as much as I've gathered."

"She was Gloria Durham, and she married Prince Antonio Della Corsini ten years ago. The usual story of a whirlwind romance in New York – he was at least twenty years her senior. After he died a few years ago, she inherited everything. We all expected her to return to New York, but she's stayed on, endearing herself even more to the locals, and, perhaps more importantly, to local officials. That's why I must tread lightly with this case."

Ruby nodded. "How did her husband die?"

Giudici grinned. "If you're thinking she bumped off her husband, as the *Americanos* would say, you're mistaken. He died in his sleep. Of natural causes."

"Hmmm..."

He held up a forestalling hand.

"Before she arrives, what else can you tell me about Vittorio?" Ruby asked.

"Unpleasant character." He scratched his chin. "Most unpleasant. As far as we can tell, he's had several identities, though Vittorio does appear to be his original last name. He ingratiates himself with the wealthy and famous all over Europe – usually the woman of the house – and gets invited there. Sometimes things vanish after his performances, and what's missing isn't part of his act. Often a lady's jewels."

"And he's never been caught?"

"That's what we're having trouble with. If he's accused of a theft – which is rare, given the wealthy's avoidance of scandal – then he moves on to his next victim."

"Does he ever try a spot of extortion?"

Giudici's face lit up. "You're a sharp one, aren't you, Miss Dove? *Sì*, we've heard rumours, but nothing's been proven. We can't tell if he simply uses extortion to protect himself as a jewel thief, or if it's a completely separate lucrative sideline. I suspect he wouldn't have lost an opportunity to do both."

"Have any of the guests told you their jewels are missing?"

"No, but that doesn't mean it hasn't happened, especially if he had damaging information. And they're certainly not going to come forward now as it's a perfect motive for murder."

Moretti materialised and bowed. "Marchesa Della Corsini."

The marchesa wore a black gown with sliver sleeves and a hem, in what was presumably a mourning gesture. She dabbed her eyes with a handkerchief and then waved it at Giudici in surrender, arms outstretched. "Commissario, but isn't it just *too* dreadful?"

Ruby muttered "selkies and kelpies" under her breath.

Playing along, Giudici rose and kissed her hand, leading her to a well-positioned chair opposite his own and Ruby's. "Thank you, Marchesa, for taking the time out of your—" he paused for a moment "—busy schedule. We have only a few questions."

She sniffed and looked up from her handkerchief, blinking at Ruby. "But Ruby, darling, what are you doing here?" Her voice held a slight edge. After what Fina and Pixley had told her about how the marchesa had smashed a vase, Ruby knew this wasn't a woman to be trifled with.

"I've asked Miss Dove and Miss Aubrey-Havelock – who had other matters to attend to – to join the investigation. In addition to her design skills, Miss Dove is an advanced amateur sleuth."

The marchesa pursed her lips, as if she were holding back a torrent of words.

Giudici ploughed forward. "Now, would you please tell us how you came to assemble this particular house party?"

"Though I've hosted many parties, I'd never hosted a masked ball. As it was dreary February and near Mardi Gras, a masked ball event seemed fun. That's why I invited Miss Dove, and her, ah, assistant, so they could design my costume."

Giudici nodded. Moretti scribbled furiously in a chair behind the marchesa.

"As for everyone else, let me think. Sergio, darling boy, insisted on hosting that rather boring conference or meeting here." She waved her handkerchief dismissively. "I agreed, saying I would gladly host anyone connected to the meeting as long as he didn't drag me into it."

Ruby held up a hand, unsure of the appropriate signal to pause the proceedings. "But Fina told me Sergio said he had never met you, and was, in fact, invited by a friend of yours."

An infectious laugh echoed around the room. "Sergio is *such* a character. And such a dear, but he's the most brazen liar that ever existed."

"Isn't he a law professor?" asked Giudici.

"Yes, that's what I said," she said with a twinkle. "I expect he had a little fun with Miss Havelock-Aubrey."

"Aubrey-Havelock," corrected Giudici.

"As I was saying, he invited guests for the Ethiopia meeting. First, Lord Mayhew, who is sweet, but can be, well, a little over-bearing and serious at times. Reminds me a little of my late husband, God rest his soul." She paused, as if waiting for condolences. When none were forthcoming, she continued. "Then Lady Asher, who I met in New York – the American woman in Parliament. She used to be such fun, but she, too, is too serious now. That's what politics will do to you. Then there's Lord Mayhew's little secretary, Emil what's-it. And Sergio's secretary, Mr Marsh. That's the extent of the Ethiopia meeting."

"And the other guests?"

"I invited Hazel Padmore to write my memoirs. I'd never met her before, but she came highly recommended," continued the marchesa, as if Hazel were a type of marmalade. "I thought the party would put me in the mood to reminisce. Oh, and Madam Zora – I'd met her in Paris at a fashion event, and had extended an open invitation to her. It seemed the best time to invite her and she was available." She smiled. "And I'd hoped to have her also design a few gowns for me, if I could get her in the right mood."

"And what about Miss Da Silva?" asked Ruby.

The marchesa's half-moon eyebrows rose, creating a clown-like effect. "I did not invite her. Marilyn – Lady Asher – invited her, though God knows why. The two of them are at each other like cats. And Iveta is simply dreadful."

Ruby bristled. She opened her mouth, but Giudici was too

quick for her. "And the staff? Gustavo Pavoni and Daria Lazzari? Have they been with you long?"

"Gustavo came on a few years ago, not too long after my husband passed away. I had to make cutbacks, so most of the maids went, and the two who stayed said the work was too difficult. I tried hiring a few day women to come in from the village, but that didn't work. So Gustavo introduced me to Daria, and she's been like the equivalent of two maids – incredibly efficient."

"How do you run such a large household with only two staff?" asked Ruby.

"Gustavo and Daria manage. And as I said, I had to make cuts somewhere."

Giudici pre-empted Ruby's next question. "But you have the money to host a ball – if you'll excuse the impertinence."

The marchesa ran her tongue along her bottom lip. "Yes, well, you have to understand something, Commissario. I grew up poor in New York City. Dirt poor. That saving mentality never leaves you, and comes in handy even when you have access to all this." She waved her hand around the room. "I make cuts in one area so I can spend lavishly in others."

He blinked. A fire spark made the marchesa jump.

He smiled and continued. "Finally, we have Vittorio and his assistant, Isa Fiore."

Moretti and Ruby leaned forward.

The marchesa leaned back and her shoulders dropped. "Ah, Vittorio. His dirty dealings finally caught up with him."

Giudici's voice rose. "Are you saying he tried to extort money from you?"

"Not tried, Commissario, he *did*. I don't mind telling you now he's dead. I assume this is all confidential." She levelled her gaze at Ruby.

"*Naturalmente*," Giudici replied. "Please, continue."

"As I said, I grew up dirt poor. But not many people are aware of that. Nor do they know about my father, who left us when I was three years old." She patted her puffy blonde hair. "Growing up poor wasn't enough for extortion, but when your father was a notorious gangster, well, then, it's another matter. His name was Bobby 'Finger' Egan."

Moretti coughed. "I've heard of him. Killed, what, at least ten people?"

"More than that, Moretti, but I cannot understand how that's relevant to the investigation. The point is, Vittorio discovered it and said if I didn't invite him this weekend, he'd send it to the newspapers. So I invited him."

"But had you met him before?" asked Ruby.

"I'd met him briefly at a friend's hunting party in Switzerland. He was charming, of course, and said we'd meet again. I didn't understand what he really meant. That was about six months ago. A few months after, he wired me, saying he'd like a chat on the phone. Though it was odd, I agreed. He laid out his terms, which included an invitation to the next house party I hosted. That was another reason I decided to have this party sooner rather than later. He promised me the party would be the end of his demands."

"And you believed him?" asked Giudici.

"What choice did I have? I suppose part of me did fantasise he'd keep his word and disappear." She chuckled. "No pun intended, but I cannot say I'm sorry he has literally disappeared off the face of this earth."

Then she leaned forward, staring at Ruby. "And I'm certain your friend, Fina, is delighted as well."

28

Giudici's crooked grin turned on an unnerved Ruby. "What does the marchesa mean, Miss Dove?"

Marchesa Gloria leaned back and crossed her arms, as satisfied as a cat who got the cream. "Why don't you tell them about Miss Aubrey-Havelock's encounter with the great magician in the cellar?"

Ruby smoothed her skirt and pulled on her earlobe. "I'm afraid you're being rather opaque, Marchesa. Would you state your case plainly?"

"Isa, Vittorio's little assistant, told me everything. She said Fina cracked him over the head with a metal pole, which is why he disappeared for a day or so."

Giudici nodded at Moretti, who scampered from the room.

The grandfather clock chimed in the corner. Ruby took a deep breath. "Vittorio was alone with Fina in the cellar, it's true. He tried to assault her, so she hit him on the head with whatever came to hand. Though she was sure she killed him – which is why she ran from the scene – he had disappeared when we returned. We couldn't understand what happened, because Fina had felt his pulse and he was quite dead. Later, Isa said he'd gone to visit a sick aunt, so we realised we'd been wrong."

Isa and Moretti stepped into the room. Isa wore a simple peasant frock. She folded her full skirts round her tightly as she sat down, revealing just how small her frame was.

"Miss Fiore. The marchesa told us you know what happened between Vittorio and Miss Aubrey-Havelock in the cellar. We'd like to hear your story."

She twisted her skirts around her finger. "There's not much to say, Commissario. Vittorio said he'd wanted to play a joke on Miss Aubrey-Havelock because she seemed like she would... how do you say? She would react."

Despite herself, Ruby smiled.

"Yes, so he said he planned a joke, thinking she would struggle or hit him if he tried to kiss her. Then he would fall to the floor, pretending he'd had a heart attack. She would think he'd died and would run from the room, terrified. Then he would disappear and she would be most distressed. He had a wicked – no, a vile sense of humour, Commissario."

"But how did he plan to stop his pulse in case she checked to see if he were alive, which she did?" asked Ruby.

Isa's ringlets shook. "He put paper bags underneath his arm – arm, armpits, yes?" She pointed to her own.

They all nodded encouragingly.

"Yes, when you put them under your armpits, it stops blood flowing to the arms – if you squeeze your armpits against your body. So you have no pulse!"

Giudici and Ruby stared at each other.

Ruby cleared her throat. "So you're saying he deliberately set her up to play this supposed joke on her?"

Isa nodded. "I'm sorry for your friend. He was a vile man."

"But why did you continue as his assistant?" The marchesa

shook her head and then covered her open mouth with her bejewelled hand. "He forced you?"

Giudici held up a forestalling hand. "Please, dear Marchesa. We'll ask the questions. First, I want to hear precisely what happened as Vittorio's joke didn't go according to plan. That is, Miss Aubrey-Havelock cracked him on the head with a pipe."

"He has a tremendously thick skull – and head," said Isa sadly. "He was injured, but not too badly. It still worked with his general plan."

The marchesa sniffed. "It does give Miss Aubrey-Havelock a motive for murder."

"How so?" asked Ruby.

"Well, she believed she'd murdered him and then he reappeared. He could have charged her with assault, couldn't he, Commissario?" She batted long false eyelashes at him.

Hmph. The woman wasn't as sharp as she'd thought.

"I cannot comprehend how it's a motive for killing him, as Miss Aubrey-Havelock had an option to claim personal defence," said Giudici. "And it's certainly no more of a motive than you have, dear lady, or you may have—" He turned to Isa. "Miss Fiore. Care to explain your employment with Vittorio?"

Isa's chin jutted upward, mirroring the marchesa's motion. "As I told Miss Dove last night, he visited my small town, Predappio, and hired me, as he was looking for a contortionist. I had been training as a gymnast."

"But last night you made it seem as if you were happy to join him," said Ruby.

Moretti's eyebrows rose.

She twisted her skirts again. "It wasn't exactly a lie. I was glad to join him, initially. But he became increasingly cruel if I made a mistake – even during our practice for the show. At first it was words, but then it became... more." She rolled up the sleeve of her frock, revealing a large, blue-black bruise.

Moretti, Ruby, and the marchesa gasped. Giudici rose and peered at the bruise closely, as if it were an unidentifiable poisonous mushroom.

He sat back down. "Now, can you tell us anything further about what happened last night? Please chime in, Marchesa, if you have anything to add."

Isa pushed down her sleeve. "After Madam Zora, Mr Marsh, Iveta, and the skeleton won the costume prizes—"

"Which skeleton?" asked Giudici.

"Someone in a skeleton costume skulked about all night. No one knows who they are," said Ruby.

"Moretti: make a note to check in town with the revellers about the skeleton."

Moretti scribbled while nodding.

"Then I introduced Vittorio," Isa went on. "He took the stage while I prepared the box. I rolled the box onstage when he called Miss Aubrey-Havelock as a volunteer."

"If you ask me, that young lady appears all too often in this scenario," interjected Marchesa Gloria.

Giudici pushed down a calming hand through the air. "Then what happened, Miss Fiore?"

"Miss Aubrey-Havelock was shaking, so I assume she was afraid Vittorio would put her in the box. I reassured her all she had to do was knock on the box and look inside. She did that and then I slipped in and *poof* – he sawed through the box."

"Please explain the trick, Miss Fiore."

She sighed. "I suppose it doesn't matter now that he's dead. When I get into the box, I pull a lever that pushes out a pair of rubber feet at the end of the box – they resemble mine. But I'm really squished into the first third of the box, so when he saws through, it's just through an empty box."

"What about the blood?" asked Ruby.

"It's simple. We put a bladder full of pig's blood in an empty cavity so it bursts when Vittorio saws through it."

The marchesa leaned forward. "Why did the lights go out?" Though Ruby expected the marchesa's questions to irritate Giudici, he merely smiled.

Isa shook her head. "I assumed it was because of the storm. But it wasn't part of the act, unless Vittorio arranged for it in secret." She sighed. "When the lights came back on, I bent over Vittorio, since he had fallen. His glassy eyes told me he was dead, so I didn't check to make sure – I just knew. After that, everything is a blur."

"The marchesa approached, and told Gustavo and Daria to leave," said Ruby.

"I told them to calm the guests and find help."

"Then Lord Mayhew, dressed as a Venetian doctor, whispered something to you, Marchesa," said Ruby.

The marchesa's half-moon eyebrows rose. She said slowly, "Yes, he did, though I had forgotten about it. He said we'd need to clear everyone from the stage."

"Then we found the syringe on the floor," said Ruby.

"I can help you with that," said a voice from the doorway.

29

Pigeons flapped and fluttered as Fina sat on a bench, contemplating Lake Como. The sun fell on her face, and the lake surface's glassy calm made her heart slow. She smiled despite herself – no reason to be anxious.

She closed her eyes, imagining their adventures since they'd met Pixley in Oxford. Where would Pixley run? If it were her, where would she run?

Noise from a nearby street turned her head. A man with an apron round his waist yelled and waved his hands. A black cat slipped between his legs and sprinted, with a fish in her mouth, toward Fina. The cat slowed to a trot as the man returned inside. After dropping the fish on the pavement, the cat gulped it down in two bites. She then casually washed her paws as if she had nothing to do with the slice of fishtail on the paving stone.

Fina stared at the fishtail. Fish. Fishing. Lake. That was it! Those little colourful fishermen's sheds on the lake. She rose, made a clucking noise over the cat – as if the cat cared – and dashed down the hill toward the lake.

The planks on the dock creaked and moaned as Fina trod lightly toward the red shed. She pressed her ear against it, hearing nothing. She tried the yellow door. Still nothing. Finally, she came to a sky-blue shed, wrinkling her nose as she approached. What was that smell? Kerosene? She tiptoed to the door and listened. At first, there was dead silence, but then she heard a shuffling, scraping noise.

Time to take a chance. "Pix, Pixley, are you there?" she whispered.

The door flung open. Pixley stood there, eyes wide and shaking.

There was no mistake about it. Pixley's brother sat on the bed.

"Madam Zora," said Giudici. "Please join our little questioning party."

Madam Zora frowned at the word 'party', but moved with her quick step toward them, settling in a chair near Isa.

"I'm sorry to disturb you, but I was passing when I heard you mention the word 'syringe'. I could not understand the rest, as English is a baffling language when she is spoken loudly enough, but nearly impossible through a door."

So Madam Zora was a snoop. Ruby should have guessed.

"Now, what's this about a syringe?" asked Giudici.

Zora coughed and opened her slim purple-grey bag. She withdrew a brown leather case and handed it to Giudici. He opened it and revealed its contents to the gathering. It held a glass syringe, with two small bottles full of liquid.

"You have arthritis, don't you, Madam Zora?" asked Ruby. "I noticed your swollen finger joints."

"You are so clever, dear. Yes, my doctor prescribes gold salt injections when the pain is insufferable."

"Did the syringe we found belong to you? That one was silver, not glass."

Zora nodded. "It was mine, I'm quite certain. Mine disappeared soon after I arrived." She shrugged. "I assumed I had forgotten it at my hotel in Paris, but I always travel with two in case one breaks. I thought nothing of it until last night, of course."

"Were your medicine bottles missing?" asked Ruby.

"No, just the syringe case. That is all."

Giudici lit another cigarette. "Why didn't you tell us earlier, Madam Zora?"

"I was afraid because I have had rather unpleasant experiences with the police in my country, you understand?"

He nodded. "What's done is done. At least you've solved the mystery of where it came from, though we still don't know who stole it."

Madam Zora smiled. "You are a good policeman, Commissario."

He turned red and said, "Do not rely on my good nature, Madam Zora. I am a professional who always finds the criminal."

Moretti nodded eagerly.

"What can you tell us about Vittorio, Madam Zora? Did you know him?"

She shook her head. Ruby paused and looked at Giudici, who hummed a tune.

"Why do I sense you're lying?" he asked.

Ruby felt she could ask her question in good conscience now. "Though I adore you, Madam Zora, it's best if you explain your relationship with Vittorio – Fina and I saw you in the cellar that day. It was quite clear you two were close, even if that was no longer the case."

She let out a long, hissing sigh. "We were lovers of a kind, a long time ago. But it was over years ago, in Kiev."

"What was he doing in Kiev?"

Zora's eyebrows rose. "In Kiev? I do not know, really... practising magic? He was always vague about what he did. I assumed it was just the magician's way."

Giudici clicked his tongue against his teeth. "So what else can you tell us about him?"

Ruby held up her hand. "But wait. It was clear from your conversation you were jealous of Isa being his young, beautiful assistant."

She shrugged. "It was more out of concern that he'd make a fool of himself, yet again."

"Who do you think killed him?" Giudici asked.

"That, Commissario, is your easiest question yet." She laughed, but the sound was harsh in the hushed room.

"Who, then?" asked Ruby, leaning forward.

"Emil Pleischner."

30

Gunmetal-blue shone up at Fina. Pixley gasped and held his hands to his mouth, moving backward toward her.

Even in this moment of unreality, Fina surveyed Pixley's brother more closely. Though he was sitting on the bed, his long legs indicated he'd be taller than Pixley. And he had hair, though it too was receding, likely in the same way Pixley's had before he'd shaved it all off. He was more thinly built, but Pixley's dimples appeared on his face when he gave them a sinister grin.

Then his mouth dropped into a grim line. "Pix, who is this woman?"

"She–she–she's Fina Aubrey-Havelock. A good friend, Shaka. You can trust her, just like you can trust me."

"After you ratted on me to the police? Not bloody likely, even if you are my brother."

"I didn't rat on you, Shaka. Would I ever do such a thing to my flesh and blood?"

"You'd sell our mother if it would get you a story for your precious newspaper," he spat out.

Pixley's mouth hung open. "Bringing Mum into this is low, even for you." He moved toward the bed.

"Stay away, and get your hands up!"

Fina and Pixley raised their hands.

Shaka paced round the small stool next to the bed. He mumbled to himself.

"Shaka, I—" pleaded Pixley.

"Quiet!"

Pixley glanced at Fina with his familiar 'I'm sorry' eyes. Fina felt preternaturally calm. So calm, in fact, that she shrugged in reply.

"I thought his name was Ernest," she said.

"It is. His middle name is Shaka – that's what he's always been called inside our family." He paused and looked at Shaka. "How did you find me and why are you here?"

Shaka and Fina began talking at once.

"Who are you asking, me or Red?" asked Shaka.

"How did you know she's called Red?" asked Pixley.

"She has reddish hair, you dunce," replied Shaka.

Pixley put down his hands. "This is rubbish, Shaka. If you want to shoot me, please do, but I will not stand here in an undignified manner, with my hands up, discussing the colour of Fina's hair."

Shaka's eyes widened. "I see you've grown, younger brother. Standing up for yourself for once, instead of falling for every shiny object in sight."

"At least it's better than being a criminal," whispered Pixley.

"What did you say?"

"Stop!" yelled Fina.

Shaka and Pixley froze.

"Enough, you two. You're just like children. Don't you know how precious it is to have a sibling – a brother? Mine was murdered and whatever's passed between you two, I know you'd cry like babies if you lost one another."

They stood in stunned silence.

"Be that as it may," said Shaka in a low voice, "We have other matters to discuss. Like where to hide."

"I'm hiding here," said Pixley. "You can find somewhere else to hide."

"No," said Shaka. "I cannot take that chance. You two must join me because I have no guarantee you won't tell the police you saw me."

"We wouldn't dare," said Pixley. "Besides, they think we're the same person, so they'll be quite pleased to prosecute me in your place."

Shaka scratched the stubble on his chin. "They think you're me? But we look different."

Pixley rolled his eyes. "Use your brain, Shaka. Remember how our teachers would mix us up all the time, as if it were that difficult to tell us apart?" He paused. "And you really need a shave. Why don't we return to the villa and sort this out? Giudici is a peculiar chap, but he seems reasonable."

Fina held up a hand as if she were in school. "I don't think that's the best idea, Pix. They'll just arrest you both, and will probably try you for the same crimes. They'll say you were accomplices."

"That's the first reasonable thing Red's said so far," said Shaka. "Look. I have a hiding place that has warmth and food," he said, eyeing the pickled vegetables doubtfully.

"Food?" asked Pixley and Fina in unison.

MORETTI CAME BACK into the Occult Room, shaking his head.

"No one can find Mr Pleischner, sir. Mr Mayhew said they'd met a few hours ago, but no one has heard from him since."

Giudici rose. "Time for a search party. We're almost finished with the questioning anyway."

A chaotic frenzy broke out at the villa, with guests and police all drawn into the drama. Slipping away from the crowd, Ruby found the servants' back stairs, near the dining room. She tiptoed down the stairs as everyone else searched the upstairs rooms. Out of the gloom appeared a well-lit corridor with two green doors. She jiggled one handle. Locked. She tried the other, but it was also locked. Ruby removed a hairpin from her pocket, bent it upward, and jammed it into the second door's keyhole.

Footsteps approached, but the echo confused the direction of the sound. She jiggled the hairpin again, but this time it dropped to the floor.

Now the footsteps couldn't be more than a minute away. Drat. She hid behind an open cupboard door.

She peered through the crack created by the cupboard's door hinge, hoping her feet were still enough to escape notice.

Isa Fiore's brow furrowed in concentration as she picked up Ruby's hairpin, examining it as if it were a precious stone. Then she jammed it into the lock and turned the knob. Presto. The door opened and Isa slipped in.

Though tempted to confront Isa – to catch her in the act – Ruby restrained herself by staring at her watch, willing the seconds to tick by.

Within less than a minute, Isa marched out, holding a leaflet in her hand. She slammed the door with her head held high, just as the butler's uniformed trousers appeared in the stairwell.

With her hands on her hips, Isa spewed a stream of Italian dialect. Even if Ruby had been able to understand it, the words were too rapid.

Gustavo's hooded eyes lowered until they were almost

closed. In a rather shocking display of non-deference, he volleyed the words right back at Isa in the same dialect.

Isa stamped her foot, turned up her nose even higher, and marched up the stairs, leaving Gustavo looking bewildered, with a slack jaw and wide eyes. He shut the door and ran up the stairs.

Breathing a heavy sigh of relief, Ruby slipped through the green door and leaned a chair against the handle, to prevent any further surprises. The room clearly belonged to a woman – Daria, presumably – given its feminine trappings of hairbrush, light makeup and frocks in the wardrobe. The only sign anyone had been in the room was the open wardrobe door. Ruby peered into the gloom, admiring the neat efficiency of the shoes lined up perfectly and the carefully pressed frocks. In a darkened corner, she spied a stack of leaflets similar in size to the one Isa had in her hand. The folded brown paper read 'Anti fasciste'.

Then Ruby felt the light touch of a tapping finger on her shoulder.

31

"How much further to go? My hands are ice," moaned Pixley as he trudged up the hill.

"You always were a complainer," huffed Shaka. He stopped and arched his back. "Not far now."

"You said that thirty minutes ago," muttered Fina into her scarf.

"What was that?"

"You said we were close thirty minutes ago." Pixley stopped and waved his arms. He caught a nearby branch with one hand, sending snow cascading onto his woollen hat.

Fina and Shaka laughed as Pixley brushed snow off his hat and neck. "Go ahead, laugh all you want. But you'll be sorry when I catch cold and die." He sneezed. "See? I become ill as we speak."

Shaka blew on his hands. "I'm just as keen to arrive as you, believe me. We're almost there, though we'll need to walk behind the skijoring course."

"Pardon?" asked Fina.

He smiled. "Skijoring – it's a Swedish sport with a skier hooked up to a horse, who pulls the skier along on flat ground."

Fina surveyed the steep, snow-covered incline. "But I thought the skiing was much farther up on Mount Primo."

"That's for downhill. This is cross-country."

The smell of horses wafted toward them before they mounted the crest of the hill.

"The stables must be nearby," said Pixley.

"That means we need to go left." Shaka pointed away from the path. "We'd better dash – who knows if anyone saw us? Not far now."

Fina closed her eyes and took a deep breath. Almost there. Her stomach rumbled and her nose was numb. But her discomfort disappeared when she contemplated what would happen to them, especially now they had vanished into the snow. Surely Pixley's brother wouldn't do anything to harm them, would he?

As she peered to the right, through a group of stables, she spied a small crowd forming around a woman on skis. Pixley glanced at Fina, clearly wondering the same thing. Should they cry out? He shook his head. It would be foolish, since they'd all end up in jail, and the police would probably pin the murder – or other crimes – on Pixley and Shaka.

Shaka gave out a little cry. A grey shack – for this time it really was a shack – stood next to a copse of trees, half covered by snow. He ran toward it and pushed against the door. Leaving the door open, he ran inside.

Somehow, it seemed to be colder inside the shack than out. Shaka said, "I must start a fire."

How could one start a fire inside without burning down the hovel?

By the time Pixley and Fina had brushed the snow off each other, Shaka had already started a fire in the tiniest wood stove Fina had ever seen. Cheerful white lace curtains lined the only window, next to a small portrait of a red bird. A narrow bed stood in one corner, opposite a table with four chairs and a large kerosene lamp. Her eyes alighted on the corner stocked with food. A few loaves of bread, dried fruit, cheese, a few bottles of wine, and foil-wrapped items that must be chocolate.

Pixley goggled. "Have you been shopping, Shaka?"

Shaka crouched near the fireplace. "I knew if I found you, we'd need ample supplies. The less we go out into the open, the better. You love to eat as much as I do."

Despite herself, Fina warmed to Shaka. Someone who bought this much food couldn't be all bad.

"Did you decorate?"

He smiled. "No, this is a ski shack. People stay here if they're up on the mountain and it's too dark to return to town."

"How do you know someone won't surprise us?" Pixley ran a finger along a chocolate bar.

"I checked. It was clear no one had been in the place for ages, so I fixed it up. But I made sure it still looked derelict from the outside." He rubbed his hands together. "I'll put on the kettle while you two fix us our lunch. I'm famished."

"THERE YOU ARE," said Giudici in a low voice.

Ruby spun round to see the crooked grin on the detective's face. The dim lighting below stairs cast a sinister shadow, high-lighting all the craggy bits of his face.

"Commissario, you gave me a fright!" she said in her most cheerful voice.

He folded his arms. "Once we began the search, I realised we had lost not one, but two guests – Mr Pleischner and yourself. After it became obvious he was nowhere about, I slipped down here, wondering if perhaps you'd had a bright idea. And here we are, you with a bright idea."

She smoothed her skirt. "Everyone assumed Emil would be upstairs, so I thought I'd do my part and search the downstairs."

"Very kind of you, I'm sure." Giudici walked to the window and peered at it, even though the drapes had been drawn. He turned his head. "And what did you find?"

"Oh, nothing. I saw this door was open so I thought I'd poke around."

"Open? Really?" He held up Ruby's hairpin, the one Isa must have dropped again.

"Well, I didn't really believe Emil would hide somewhere and leave the door unlocked, so I availed myself of the opportunity to use my hairpins in service of the cause."

"Very good of you, Miss Dove. But I don't believe you didn't find anything. What were you reading?"

Moretti popped his head round the door, simultaneously frightening Ruby out of her wits and calming her nerves now that someone else was here.

"Commissario, come quickly! We've made a discovery in the cellar."

RUBY SIGHED. Here she was again, in front of the cursed tunnel. The rest of the household, minus Fina and Pixley, milled around the cellar as Moretti and Giudici conferred in the corner.

Using this opportunity to mend fences with Hazel, Ruby leaned over and said in a conspiratorial tone, "Why are we here? Where does that tunnel lead?"

Hazel scowled, but then her brow smoothed. "Moretti found this tunnel and thinks Emil disappeared into it. But why would Emil disappear?"

"They think he's the murderer."

Hazel let out a tiny halting laugh, though it was still loud enough to turn heads.

"I've never heard anything so ridiculous," she added. "Emil? A murderer? I'd sooner nominate my own grandmother as suspect number one."

Using this cosy conversation to her advantage, Ruby asked, "So, who did murder Vittorio?"

"If you ask me, it's one of those aristocrats – they're so shifty. And they're so casual about human life, it would be easy for them to do it."

"But you don't have any evidence of which one."

"No, but my money's on Lady Asher. Tough as old boots. She'd slit a competitor's throat without thinking twice. She's the kind to fire a maid because she didn't boil her egg for precisely six minutes."

Madam Zora hobbled over, as if she were still in her Baba Yaga costume. "What are you ladies discussing? The murderer?"

"We don't believe Emil is the murderer, do you?"

Ruby wasn't sure if she should be pleased or irritated Hazel used 'we'.

Madam Zora bit her lip. "No. Emil seems a sweet person – he even helped me with my costume when I became tangled in my wig." She paused. "No, I think it was Sergio."

This time, Hazel broke into a full-throated laugh, as if she'd been a heavy smoker during her short life.

Madam Zora's chin raised. "Why are you laughing at me?"

Hazel put a hand in front of her face. "I'm terribly sorry – I was just laughing at the idea Sergio could have committed a murder. He's a bit of a scamp, yes, but he's as soft as butter underneath."

Ruby bit back a retort with some effort. "Hazel thinks it's the marchesa, Lord Mayhew, or Lady Asher – most likely Lady Asher. What do you think?"

She shook her head. "No. *Nyet.*"

"Well?" asked Hazel.

"It is that little contortionist. She was abused by Vittorio and she had her revenge."

Moretti clapped his hands. "Ah, *ladies and gentlemen.*" Silence fell.

Giudici coughed. "We believe Mr Pleischner fled through this tunnel to escape his arrest. We ask you to remain here in case he returns this way. Will you do that for us?"

Lord Mayhew stepped forward and cleared his throat. "I must protest, Commissario. Emil Pleischner is a trusted and valuable employee. I—"

Giudici held up a hand. "Please, Lord Mayhew. There will be time for character witnesses later, but now we must move with all speed." His head bobbed and weaved. "Ah! Miss Dove. Please come with us, if you will."

Ruby stepped forward, ignoring the looks of envy, consternation, and puzzlement on the faces around her.

Fortunately she'd already changed her shoes.

32

Fina's head tilted forward and then whipped upright. Soft snores came from the bed where Pixley lay. Shaka's eyelids closed and then shot up again.

"What was in that food?" asked Fina in a hushed voice.

Shaka smiled. "Nothing, I expect. It's the combination of shock, exhaustion, warmth, and a decent meal." He held up a pillow. "Would you like this?"

She shook her head. "No, thank you. I'll try to push through it, though I'm not sure what I'm pushing through to. What will happen next?"

The shed began to vibrate. She swore it began to bounce.

Pixley snorted as he bolted upright. "What happened?"

Pots rattled as a loud thumping, galloping noise became louder and then died away.

"What in heaven's name was that?" roared Pixley.

"Skijoring. Here." Shaka rose and opened the door. "Come see."

Shivering, Pixley and Fina peeked out of the front door. In the distance, they saw a grey horse. Behind it was a person on skis.

"So what?" said Pixley. "It's just a person skiing behind a horse. Close the door. It's freezing!"

"So impatient, Pix," said Shaka. "Wait till they come closer."

The horse approached, and the crockery rattled. Fina's eyes widened. "The horse is dragging the skier!"

"Well, not exactly dragging," said Shaka. "As I said before, they tie a rope round the horse and the skier. Then the horse pulls them along." He shut the door. "We'd better close it before the skier sees us."

Fina waited for the galloping to subside. "Seems like the perfect sport."

"I agree," sighed Pixley. "If I were going to ski, I'd like to be towed by an animal doing all the work for me."

Shaka laughed. "It's not as easy as it looks. It takes some skill, and it can be quite dangerous if something startles the horse."

"Mmmm... I can see it all now," said Pixley. "Lady Asher tangled in in skijoring harness, just like she was tangled in scandal. Great headline."

"What scandal?" asked Fina.

"The Frobisher affair," said Shaka.

Pixley's mouth dropped open. "How did you know about that?"

"I don't live under a rock. I do read newspapers, dear brother. And from what I heard from a friend, she was in it neck-deep. She kept her seat in Parliament by bribing a few well-placed clerks to keep quiet."

"This is a great story!" Pixley rummaged in his bag and withdrew a pencil and notepad.

"Pix," said Fina. "Have you forgotten what's happening? We're being held captive by your brother while the police are searching for you in connection with a murder. It's hardly the time to be thinking about a newspaper story."

As if in answer to Fina's warning, someone thumped on the door.

"You must be joshing," said Ruby.

"I'm afraid not, Miss Dove." Giudici swung his leg over the bicycle seat. "Are you coming with us?"

"But how will we see? The tunnel is dark for miles." She reluctantly pulled up her skirt and gently slid onto the seat.

"How did you know that?" He smiled.

"I just assumed a tunnel like this would be long and dark." She smiled back sweetly.

He cleared his throat. "Moretti is a good chap, as you English would say. He's procured these helmets from the costume room." He pointed at three ridiculous Roman helmets Moretti was fiddling with. "And he's attaching torches to each helmet so we'll all be able to see."

"Splendid," deadpanned Ruby. "What do we hope to accomplish? That we'll apprehend Emil because he'll be so overcome with laughter when he sees us he'll be unable to run?"

"Droll, very droll, Miss Dove. So glad you have a sense of humour. Here." He gave her a helmet and she slid it onto her head. It was too large, however, so she had to push it back, also pushing back the torch so it lit the ceiling instead of the passage.

"Just follow us, Miss Dove. We have enough light for all of us. We must move quickly before night falls outside the tunnel."

They pedalled until they came to the stairs. Moretti hoisted each of their bicycles up the stairs and they were off again. After a while, the flat surface began to climb, and cold air seeped in through the walls. Ruby was glad they had been pedalling for so long she was warm enough to keep going. Moretti looked back and stopped. He climbed off his bike and handed Ruby his coat.

She shook her head and smiled. "*Grazie*. I'm warm enough." He smiled, shrugged, and they continued.

"Not much farther now!" called Giudici. "The marchesa said the opening should be in a few minutes."

A halo of light shone from the ceiling. "It's the opening!" cried Giudici. He slid off his bike and let it fall to the floor.

Ruby followed suit, though she parked her bicycle against the tunnel wall. Moretti did the same and motioned to her to go first.

"Wait," said Giudici. "I'll climb up first to make sure everything is safe. Then, Moretti, you'll assist Miss Dove up and then you go last."

"I'm sure I can manage," said Ruby, though her legs felt like rubber from the ride.

"As you wish." He gripped the metal ladder rungs along the wall and propelled himself upward. He pushed and pushed with his head and neck against a round trapdoor in the ceiling. She heard a satisfying popping noise as he finally succeeded, disappearing into the twilight above.

She steadied herself on the bottom rung and climbed upwards, glad she did not have to lift the trapdoor herself. The soft blue-pink-gold light of twilight would have been enchanting had it not been for their task. The bare trees stretched toward the sky as if pleading for a little more sunlight on a winter's day. Ruby pulled herself up with one hand, giving the other to Giudici, somehow avoiding soiling her lovely coat on the snow and mud. Giudici blew on his hands and stamped his feet as they waited for Moretti to join them.

Giudici pointed in the distance at a horse galloping toward them.

"Is that a person behind it? On skis?" asked Ruby.

Giudici muttered some unintelligible oath in Italian as he helped Moretti from the tunnel.

"Now," he said. "Let's find Pleischner."

"Commissario." Moretti pointed. "Shall we try there?"

A dilapidated shack stood in the distance.

Giudici snorted. "Good idea, Moretti, but no one's been in that shack for years. I doubt anyone would survive opening the door – the place would surely cave in."

"I'm not so sure, Commissario," said Ruby. "Do you see the smoke coming from the chimney?"

33

The trio froze. Pixley and Fina looked toward Shaka, whose face was perfectly calm.

Shaka lifted his chin toward Fina.

She nodded and went to the door. "Who is it?"

"*Bitte*, please, I am freezing. *Helfen!*"

She mouthed to Pixley and Shaka, "Pleischner."

Pixley shrugged. Shaka opened the door to a shivering, hunched-over Emil. Snow covered his bald head and eyebrows, turning him into a snowman.

"*Bitte*." His teeth chattered as Shaka grabbed him by the shoulder and shoved him into the hovel, but not before checking around outside, presumably to make sure this wasn't a setup.

Pixley brushed away the snow covering Emil, while Fina put a pot of water on the stove.

"Here, get his clothes off," said Shaka.

Pixley and Fina stared at Shaka.

"He's going to freeze to death if we don't get him warm, and we certainly can't do that with these clothes." He pulled off Emil's jacket and began to unbutton his shirt.

"But there's a lady present," said Pixley.

"You always were a fool, Pix, but I suppose it's good to be reminded. The man will die if we don't get him warm. Do you understand?"

Pixley nodded and helped his brother disrobe Emil.

Fina turned away and stared out of the little window. "What will you put on him to warm up?"

"Blankets, of course," said Shaka.

"No, I mean, it will take ages for his clothes to dry," said Fina.

"I have an idea!" cried Pixley. In the window's reflection, Fina saw Pixley stripping as well.

"Pix, we can't have two freezing people. One is more than enough," growled Shaka.

"No, no. You'll see." Pixley held up his long underwear. "I knew they'd come in handy, even though Fina and Ruby mocked me for wearing them."

"Excellent, dear brother. Glad to see you can snap out of your stupidity once in a while."

"Hey! Stop the insults. They're not helping."

"I'll tell you what's not helping," said Fina.

Shaka and Pixley stopped. Emil looked up in a stupor.

"Someone's coming on foot. Not by skis. There are three of them."

"Can you tell who it is?"

Fina squinted and her stomach churned.

"Giudici, Moretti, and Ruby."

"*ANDIAMO*." Giudici waved them toward the shack. "Emil must be hiding in there. We'll get him now."

Ruby hung back a moment, sensing she shouldn't go on. "I'll wait here – I'll just be in your way."

Giudici's eyes narrowed and then he shrugged. They trudged toward the shack.

Ruby shivered and rubbed her arms. Out of the corner of her eye, she spied a flash of black against the white snow. A horse galloped toward her, but unlike the other horse, this one was on its own, with no skier trailing along behind it. The horse ran as if it had been startled, perhaps explaining why she had lost her passenger.

Ruby cooed, "*Calma, calma.*"

To her utter surprise, the horse slowed and approached her. She patted the horse's nose, stroking the white star on her forehead. "Hullo, sweetie, what's your name? Stella, I think."

Stella lifted her head toward the shack. Ruby turned her head and saw Emil running in the snow, flapping about in long underwear two sizes too large for him. Moretti and Giudici pursued him, though they had a rough time of it in the snow. Emil looked like a bird with a broken wing.

"Come on, Stella." Ruby hoisted herself onto Stella, half-on, half-off, gripping her mane with all her might. But Stella didn't complain. When Ruby was finally on the horse, but unable to sit up, she gave Stella a gentle pat. "Go on, sweetheart." And Stella trotted toward the shack, snuffling and snorting as she went. When they were near the shack, Ruby said, "Whoa," and Stella obeyed.

Ruby slipped off the horse and opened the door to a wide-eyed Fina, Pixley, and, judging by his appearance, Pixley's brother.

"Just raise your hands, please."

Pixley's brother trained his gun on Ruby.

"Put the blasted gun down, you idiot," said Pixley. "Someone's bound to be hurt. This is Ruby Dove, you oaf."

"I don't know who Ruby Dove is, but I do know she came with the lillies, which sets her far back in my book, Pix."

"Please, Shaka, put the gun down," pleaded Fina, wondering what 'lillies' meant. Then she realised it was the police.

"Quiet, Fina. Let me think."

"I came on a lovely horse named Stella," said Ruby in a low voice, still holding her hands high. "I'm sure she'll take you wherever you want to go."

"Ruby Dove!" yelled Fina and Pixley in unison.

"Thanks, Miss Dove," smiled Shaka. "You're not so bad after all."

He slipped out into the night.

34

"Ruby, my precious, but we were so anxious for your health!"
Iveta enfolded Ruby in a red-and-orange froth of nonsense, as
Pixley had lovingly termed Iveta's costumes.

A twittering, excited chatter broke out among the assembled
crowd in the dining room. Sergio blew smoke rings upward and
laughed at Hazel's witty remarks, while Madam Zora waved her
hands at Pixley. Isa stared at Daria as she slid another tray of
olive oil, bread, cheese, and olives across the table. Lady Asher
and Lord Mayhew had their heads together in an unexpectedly
cosy chat. The marchesa's eyes threw daggers in their direction.

Fina stabbed a roasted vegetable and hoisted it onto her slice
of bread. As she sank her teeth into it, she watched Puffy the cat
glide in, unnoticed, and pilfer a sardine at the far end of the
table. She and the cat were the only ones interested in food,
which she was glad of as she was interested in eating everything
in sight. Except the sardines.

The general atmosphere of bonhomie evaporated when
Emil appeared in handcuffs, though he was now wearing his
own clothes, thank goodness. Moretti's mouth was set in a grim
line, while Giudici's crooked smile made the pair look like a

comedy duo. Gustavo loomed up behind them, shoulders drooped in resignation.

Giudici stepped forward. "Ladies and gentlemen." He coughed. "If I may have your attention, I'd like to review the case so you may all return home soon."

The excited twitter returned, louder than before.

He waved his hands up and to the side, as if he were a conductor bringing a concert to its close. "Though I haven't asked her, I'd like Miss Dove and her friends to assist me in clearing up several lingering threads."

Though Ruby's eyes doubled in size, she nodded, as did Pixley and Fina.

Lady Asher coughed. "Pardon, Commissario, but I must ask why Mr Marsh is not also in handcuffs. I'd heard he's a thief."

Fina's eyes narrowed and her shoulders tensed. She opened her mouth but Pixley held up a hand. "The commissario has been good enough to allow me to explain now, as he had other matters to attend to." He nodded at Emil, who sat hunched over on a nearby chair. Fina couldn't bear to look at him.

"Yes, Mr Marsh – Mr Hayford, pardon – please take this opportunity to explain yourself," said Giudici.

Pixley removed a tiny folded slip of paper from his red jumper's slit pocket and handed it to Giudici. Giudici shook his head and handed it back. "Please read it aloud."

"I, Ernest Shaka Alain Hayford, hereby declare I am the brother of one Pixley Isaka Hayford. I have enclosed a photo of us as children to verify we are brothers and two separate people. As for the charge of being a thief, my brother may be cleared of all wrongdoing, with the enclosed newspaper clipping verifying he was in Paris last year when a major jewel robbery took place in Madrid. I take responsibility for being a part of that heist. This should therefore end any speculation about my brother's activities. Yours very sincerely, etcetera."

Pixley handed the photo and clipping to Giudici, who took time to inspect them carefully.

Lord Mayhew cleared his throat. "If I may, Inspector – ah, Commissario – I'm baffled as to why we're all here. Though I strongly disagree with your conclusions about Emil, you've clearly settled on him as the murderer, and I, for one, have urgent business in London."

Fina's jaw dropped. Ruby gripped a chair. Pixley wiped his head.

Iveta rose. "You unspeakable little man! You'd let a man who worked so hard for you go to prison because you have *business* in London? It's outrageous behaviour, even for a politician."

Everyone's head turned toward Mayhew. Even Lady Asher looked shocked. Mayhew's face turned that unlovely shade of puce again. Everyone watched in silence as he fumbled for his box of pills.

"Let us begin with Lord Mayhew, shall we?" said Giudici. "You are mistaken – fortunately, as I like Emil personally – about his guilt."

"Then why have you clapped him in irons?" asked Fina.

"It's for his protection, I assure you, Miss Aubrey-Havelock."

Fina snorted. Perhaps she had overestimated the commissario's humanity.

Giudici turned back to the crowd and hummed. "Lord Mayhew, please explain how you came to be here this weekend."

Mayhew's face had turned back to its normal ruddy shade. "Quite simple. Sergio Chapman and I had met up at Cambridge and he invited me to these Ethiopia negotiations. He knew I had expertise and interest in the matter."

"Did you know Vittorio?"

Mayhew's pills rattled in his pocket as he shifted in his seat. "No, I did not."

"That's not exactly true, is it, Lord Mayhew?" said Ruby quietly.

Everyone's head turned to the opposite end of the room.

"What do you mean?" blustered Mayhew.

"You were at the same house party a few months ago."

"What house party?" he asked.

Madam Zora jumped up. "Yes. I remember now! He was at the Duke of Perthshire's weekend shooting party."

"And how do you know that, Madam Zora?" asked Giudici quietly.

A deadly little silence ensued.

"Well, I was there, wasn't I?"

"What was the nature of your relationship with Vittorio, Madam Zora?"

"I already told you. Or I should say I told Ruby in that writing exercise we had after the murder."

"You wrote he was just an acquaintance, but that was a lie, wasn't it, Madam Zora?" asked Ruby.

"No, no. That's not true."

Fina brushed crumbs from her skirt. "Why deny it? Ruby and I overheard you two in the cellar, remember? Sounded like a lover's quarrel – you were jealous of Isa being his new assistant."

Madam Zora's tight face loosened. Then she burst out laughing, doubling over and wiping her eyes. "You two have the confidence of youth, don't you? You think anyone over thirty-five is a doddering fool."

Giudici hummed. Looking exasperated, Moretti said, "*Per favore,* Madam Zora, why are you laughing?"

"It was all part of a practical joke Vittorio planned. He wanted to trick one of the young ladies, so he gave me a general script to follow. I enjoy jokes, so I went along with it. How could I know there'd be any harm in it?"

Ruby tapped her teeth. "Excellent diversion tactics, Madam

Zora. But I'm afraid it won't work this time. Much like you believe we think you're an idiot, you think the same about us."

"Dear Miss Dove, please tell us what you're talking about. The tension is too much for my delicate nerves," said Sergio, smiling at Hazel as she chuckled at his comments about nerves.

Ruby nodded at Moretti, who stationed himself by the door. She squared her shoulders.

"Mr Chapman, we've all been taken in by a very clever piece of misdirection. It's time the truth came out. Madam Zora—" she waved a hand at the astonished designer "—is a jewel thief."

35

"You have no proof!" Madam Zora spat out.

Ruby shook her head sadly. "No, I don't, but it won't take long for Italian police to confer with London about matching up dates. But you incriminated yourself by admitting you were at the Duke of Perthshire's weekend party with Vittorio and Lord Mayhew. You told me the Duchess had taught you an English idiom, remember?"

"But Ruby, how did you know she was a jewel thief?" asked Pixley.

"I thought it was odd she could afford diamond earrings and an emerald ring. You might all think it was part of being a glamorous designer, but I knew better. She'd come from poverty and I know designers actually make very little money."

"They were gifts from rich ladies." Zora hopped up and paced back and forth.

"That may well be," said Ruby. "But after I heard about Vittorio's sideline in jewellery theft, put together with your close relationship and jewels, I knew all three together could not be a coincidence."

Moretti whispered in Giudici's ear. Giudici looked up.

"Moretti thinks you killed Vittorio in a clever double bluff, with your syringe."

"How so?" she said in a quiet voice. Fina had never seen the terrier-like Zora so calm before.

Moretti whispered again. Giudici said, "Vittorio was about to be exposed, or to expose you both, for your involvement in jewel theft, so he had to be killed. You used the syringe, put some poison on the mask as a blind, and then pretended to be worried when we discovered the syringe belonged to you."

"I'm so sorry, Madam Zora," said Ruby. "But I knew the police would latch on to you as a killer sooner rather than later – precisely because of the syringe – so I had to expose your, ah, activities to protect you. I know you're not a murderer."

"Ruby, dear girl, I'm a Cambridge professor and I cannot follow your logic. Please explain," said Sergio.

"Consider the full import of killing a man like Vittorio. The question we should ask about Madam Zora is not when or how she might have killed Vittorio, but *why*?"

Lord Mayhew said, "But Moretti just explained that she would have to kill him if he were about to expose their jewel thefts."

Giudici nodded. "I think I understand Miss Dove's point about Madam Zora not being the killer. It's true she'd need to silence him, but killing him would likely reveal his thirst for jewels during an investigation. She might escape notice if she were not present at the time of the murder, but she'd be exposed as a thief during the murder inquiry."

"But was she, as you say, exposed, Commissario?" Sergio winked at Hazel – somewhat inappropriately given the situation, Fina thought.

"No, though it's been a rather unconventional investigation, even for a homicide."

Iveta raised a hand. "Darlings, I've had a thought. Since

Madam Zora is not a killer, I have a further question about the jewels – you understand it is my business."

Fina nodded. "If I may, Iveta?"

"Of course, my little one. Please go on. I am tired of English today."

"At lunch on the first day, Miss Da Silva remarked on Lady Asher's fake pearls. Miss Da Silva can identify a fake at fifty paces, I'm sure."

Iveta dazzled them with her broad smile. Lady Asher's face turned translucent. She wiped the corners of her mouth absently.

"So the question is whether Madam Zora replaced Lady Asher's pearls with paste."

"That is out of the question," piped up the marchesa. "I know about fake jewels due to some, ah, previous connections. And unless Madam Zora had seen the pearls before, it would take time to make a replica. Even if she had paste pearls approximately the same size, she'd need to make the string the exact same length as the necklace, which also wouldn't be that simple."

Iveta nodded. "I must admit the marchesa is correct."

"What about Vittorio?" asked Hazel. "Couldn't he have seen the pearls before?"

"Yes, how about it, Marilyn? Do you want to incriminate yourself?" Sergio cracked a smile. Fina felt like kicking him, even though she had no fondness for Lady Asher.

Lady Asher folded her hands in her lap, though Fina saw a forefinger shake. "I'd never met Vittorio before this weekend."

"What about the pearls, Lady Asher? I'm sorry, but I must ask," said Giudici quietly.

"They are an imitation, yes. I had to pawn them and hoped no one would notice. No one did notice, until Iveta had the temerity to say it in public. I was so ashamed."

Iveta rose. "It is my profession, and I am sorry I embarrassed you. It was not my intention. But you have dismissed me ever since I arrived, treated me as a 'foreigner' as they say, even though you invited me to help you!" She raised a finger in the air in an unfortunate mimicry of one of Il Duce's impassioned speeches.

Sergio let out a low whistle. Hazel put a hand on his arm.

Lady Asher buried her face in her well-manicured hands. "I haven't any money. Ever since the Frobisher affair, when I invested all the money my husband left me, I've been flat broke. I had to pawn the beautiful pearls. And I thought I could move to Brazil – or Argentina – and live on a small allowance."

"Hmph," said Iveta. "That is why she invited me here. But when she realised it would take money to get her to Brazil, she turned ice cold – which is in keeping with her general personality. I should have known after that weekend in Wiltshire."

"You never had a chance to tell me what happened, Iveta," said Ruby.

Iveta let out a great sigh. "I was invited by the Duke – or was it Lord – of Wiltshire to a weekend party. He wanted me to value some of his wife's jewels. Somehow, Lady Asher discovered my profession and started to tell all the guests about it. Now, word-of-mouth discussion is important for my profession, but discussing it openly in mixed company is, well, too vulgar. Besides, she began to refer to me as 'the jewel lady', which was just too much."

"I must say it doesn't sound like the Marilyn I know," said Sergio. "Too tight-lipped for such frivolities."

"You are quite right, Mr Chapman. But she had been drinking."

36

A silence fell.

As if he could make up for his gaffe, Sergio said cheerfully, "And what about you, Miss Da Silva? You and Vittorio were in the same line."

Iveta loomed over Sergio. "Same line? Same line? How dare you!"

Ruby reached out and put a firm hand on her shoulder. "He is being insulting, dear Iveta, but you'd better explain your relationship."

Iveta's shoulders drooped and she sat back down in her regal chair. "As I've already revealed, I knew Vittorio – though not that well – more by his reputation. He practised extortion on well-to-do ladies, and also stole their jewels. Though I admit I wished he would truly vanish like he had in one of his acts, I had no wish to do him harm."

"But why not?" asked Hazel. "Wasn't he muddying the waters for you? Weren't you afraid the two of you would become associated with one another?"

Iveta rearranged the folds of her magnificent tulle gown.

"Three reasons, *dear* Miss Padmore. First, if I were to kill Vittorio, I would do so in a rage. This elaborate planning charade–" she wagged a finger "–no, it is not for me. A pistol. Or a knife, yes, a knife right to the heart. That would be me."

"But perhaps it's all part of an act," said Hazel.

Pixley snorted.

"As you can see by Mr Marsh's reaction, I cannot hide who I truly am. This is Iveta Da Silva in her full glory. Take it or leave it, as some English-speakers say."

"And the second and third reasons?" asked Isa.

"Ah, the little contortionist speaks! The second reason is I avoid police involvement at all costs. I am always strictly legal, of course—" she glanced at Giudici "—but police involvement is never good for my reputation, as my ladies and lords demand discretion. I've already been involved in one unfortunate incident in Lisbon, and I've had to explain it away to many ladies who have contacted me."

"And the third, Iveta?" asked Pixley.

"Ah, dear Pixley. You'll know the third reason better than anyone, except perhaps the charming Miss Aubrey-Havelock." She paused, for full theatrical effect. "The third reason is Ruby Dove."

All eyes stared at Ruby. For the first time, Fina sensed by Ruby's downcast eyes that she was uncomfortable with the attention. Then she rallied, raised her chin and smiled at Iveta.

"I would never try to murder or steal anything in front of the magnificent Miss Dove." She waved a finger at each person in the room. "But one of you certainly tried."

Sergio stood up. "Well, I'll be off. We've solved the jewel thefts and we have the murderer in custody." He pointed at Emil.

"Sit down, Mr Chapman," said Giudici quietly.

"Why?"

"We're not finished."

Lady Asher's mouth curved in a cruel smile. She had revived. "While we're at it, dear Sergio, tell us why you're such a compulsive liar."

Sergio's smirk disappeared. "Whatever do you mean?"

"I heard about your little charade on the lake. Where you said someone pushed you in."

"He wasn't lying," said Fina. "He really was pushed into the lake – I was there."

"Was he pushed, or did he fall on purpose?" asked Lady Asher.

Hazel became indignant. "Why would he lie?"

"Because he wanted to pretend someone threatened his life," said Ruby.

"But why?" asked the marchesa.

"Perhaps to give leverage with the negotiations, somehow," said Ruby. She looked at Pixley. "Any ideas, Pix?"

Pixley pursed his lips, held his breath, and then let out a stream of air. "Kind of you, Ruby, to believe in the old noggin, but I'm afraid I'm fresh out of ideas."

"Fina, can you remind us who was on the ferry who is also here, in this room?"

Fina squeezed her eyes shut. "Well, besides myself and Sergio, there was the man in the brown suit – Lord Mayhew – and Emil, though I didn't see him."

"See?" said Sergio. "It was Emil. It all ties together."

"But he has no reason to kill you, Sergio," said Ruby. "No, it was much more complex. You knew Lord Mayhew was on the ferry and you wanted leverage against him in the negotiations on behalf of Ethiopia. After all, he was the only one who was for letting the Italians remain in Ethiopia – or, in the best-case scenario, handing it over to the British."

"What utter rot, dear girl," said Sergio. "It was clearly Lord Mayhew who killed Vittorio."

"He doesn't have a motive, dear boy," said Hazel.

Lord Mayhew wiped his forehead. "I didn't want to say anything to jeopardise the negotiations, but it's true. After the incident on the ferry, Sergio said he'd tell everyone I'd pushed him in to kill him to stop or stall the negotiations. He said he had all those witnesses."

"Is he mad?" asked Lady Asher.

Hazel looked at her increasingly agitated companion and stroked his arm. "Shhh... Sergio. It will be alright."

Pixley's eyes goggled. "Are–are you saying that he's...?"

"Will someone tell me what's going on?" asked the marchesa, whose eyebrows had risen to a level Fina had never seen before.

Ruby whispered into Hazel's ear. Hazel nodded and said, "I suppose I'd better tell you all. It's not easy, after all this time, but..." She took a deep breath. "Sergio is my brother – half-brother, that is. We share the same mother. He's always been brilliant, a genius, but he's always tended toward a fantasy world when he's under stress. He's been under a great deal of strain for a while, and seems to have been worse since we've travelled here. Perhaps it's the stress of the negotiations. I thought leaving Cambridge would make him better."

"So he's barmy," Pixley said, more to himself than to anyone else. He looked down at his knees and removed his glasses to wipe his eyes, drying what Fina thought must be incipient tears.

"Not barmy, Pixley, just a little stressed, that's all," said Hazel.

Fina held up a finger. "Wait. Now I realise who it was on the phone the night Vittorio died. When Ruby, Pixley, and I were going to the kitchen, I tripped, knocked over the telephone, and then heard someone say 'Gattara' on the phone. It must have been Sergio."

Giudici, Moretti, Daria, and Gustavo broke into laughter.

"*Gattara* means an old lady who loves cats. Slightly barmy, as your friend Mr Marsh would say," said Giudici.

Sergio's face was blank. Hazel looked up. "It was Sergio – it was his code name for you, Fina, since you love cats."

"Why was he talking about me? And why on the phone?"

"He had become obsessed with you. Not in a romantic way – that was with Pixley. No, he was convinced you were some sort of grand ringleader of a fantasy gang he had created in his head."

The corner of Ruby's mouth lifted in a smile. Fina's stomach turned, not so much from the thought of Sergio's obsession, but from the way everyone was staring at her. But she felt oddly pleased at being viewed as a ringleader, even if it were by a fantasist.

"Hazel," said Ruby quietly. "You'd better explain how you came to be here."

Hazel nodded, on the verge of tears. "I knew Sergio needed to get away. When he told me about the negotiations, I said I'd go with him – he didn't know I wanted to watch over him. We concocted a scheme to have me invited. It wasn't difficult, since I am a professional writer."

"I have one more question for Hazel," said Fina. "Why were you constantly checking your watch that first day we arrived?"

Hazel gave her a wan smile. "I was worried about Sergio missing his medication. He wasn't staying on schedule while travelling, so I didn't want to miss the next dose." She rose. "Commissario, may I have permission to take Sergio upstairs to his room? I'm afraid if he remains he may become worse."

As if on cue, Sergio leapt out of his seat and pointed at Fina. "You! You've been out to get me since the beginning. Ever since that first day on the ferry." He turned around in a slow-moving circle. "You've all been out to get me. I must hide. I—"

Hazel pulled on Sergio's sleeve, making a gentle shushing noise.

Giudici scratched his head. "I need Moretti here." He scanned the room. Then he whispered to Moretti, who left the room. "We have a man on guard outside – we'll have him stand outside Mr Chapman's door to ensure he doesn't wander off."

37

Fina rose, breaking the silence that fell after Hazel and Sergio departed. "I have a question for you all. One that's been baffling, though I'm sure Ruby already knows the answer."

"Then why doesn't she tell you?" asked Lord Mayhew. "Aren't you close friends?"

"Ruby plays things close to her chest. Besides, it's always better if the person implicated explains themselves directly." Fina waved a scrap of paper about. "Someone left this note in my room. It says 'save me' on it. My passport also went missing. And I also caught someone going into my room last night. All three events must be connected."

Silence.

"Your trust in human honesty is admirable, Fina, and it's one of the reasons you're my friend. Unfortunately, we must give this person a nudge." Ruby levelled her gaze at Isa. "You already told the police you were afraid of Vittorio – that he abused you."

Iveta gasped and clicked her tongue.

"So it would be natural to try to escape. Perhaps you thought a plea would be enough, though it was so vague I don't know how you expected Fina to help you."

Isa folded her legs underneath her. "I lost my nerve that first day. I was going to write more, but I heard people in the corridor. And then I thought Vittorio might find out. He had me imagining he could see through walls. I started to believe he was magical – though not in a positive way."

"So you left the note! And my passport?" asked Fina, relieved this might be the solution to her problem.

"I'll return it. We're the same height and I thought I could dye my hair. Then I would escape somewhere, away from Vittorio." She paused. "I was also the one who entered your room that night."

"But you were free!" said Fina. "He had just died. Why would you need to go into my room again?"

"I tried to return your passport, but you discovered me before I had time to leave it."

"Is that why you were acting so peculiar in the corridor that day when you were supposedly coming from the bathroom?"

She nodded.

"Again, Miss Fiore," said Giudici, "this only strengthens your motive for murder."

"I just remembered you said your mother was a nurse in the war," blurted Fina. "That might mean you knew how to handle syringes and poisons."

Isa's eyes widened. "Why? If one's father is a shoemaker, does one automatically know how to make shoes?"

"She does have a point, Miss Fiore. You had means, motive, opportunity," said Giudici.

"And you were sweating profusely onstage, before Vittorio died," said Ruby.

"My Pierrette costume was pretty, but devilishly hot. Because Vittorio said he didn't feel well, I had to do more work, so I became overheated."

"But you were more than overworked and overheated, Isa,"

said Fina quietly. "When I saw you onstage, you were nervous. Why? You must have performed that trick many times."

"I believe you call it a premonition in English. I had a premonition something would go wrong."

"Liar!" screamed Daria as she set down a tray of biscuits.

Gustavo rushed to her side and put his arms on her shoulders. "*Calma. Calma.*" He whispered something into her ear.

Daria's blonde hair flew about like it had a life of its own. "*Fascista! Traditrice!*"

As Gustavo calmly but firmly pushed Daria into a nearby chair, Ruby moved forward.

"As Daria has revealed her motive, I can speak about it now. She has also revealed Isa's final motive, which is cooperation with the authorities."

Giudici looked up. "Authorities? She's hardly been cooperative with us."

"I mean the *carabinieri* – the national police. The first hint was when she said she was from Predappio near Bologna."

"That's where Mussolini is from," said Giudici.

"Correct," said Ruby. "That made me wonder if she knew people with great influence in the government. Perhaps enough influence to help her get out of the country, or at least out of her situation with Vittorio."

"How does this relate to Daria?" asked Pixley.

"After Fina spied a bit of newsprint in her cap, I thought there was more to Daria than met the eye. I went to her room while everyone else was busy with the search for Emil. To my surprise, Isa also searched Daria's room. I took the opportunity to sleuth as well, hoping I'd discover what Isa was after." She pulled out a leaflet from her clutch and handed it around the room.

"So that's it," said Giudici. "We already suspected there were anti-fascists in the villa, though we couldn't figure out the source."

"In my house?" The marchesa looked scandalised, though Fina thought she heard a hint of irony in her voice.

Gustavo coughed. "I will not deny it as you found the information in her room. Daria is involved, but I will say no more than that." He stroked her shoulder.

"Are you lovers?" fluted Iveta from the corner.

Lord Mayhew and Lady Asher looked as embarrassed as if they had been asked the question.

Gustavo's eyelids flickered and he smiled. "No, but we are close friends – we have worked together in many places. I helped Daria find the job here, only to realise she was involved in a dangerous game."

"But what does this have to do with Isa? She's a fascist, Daria is an anti-fascist. So what?" asked the marchesa.

"Isa was probably told by the *carabinieri* she had to produce evidence or, better yet, an actual anti-fascist for prosecution. It was her ticket out of the country, or, as I said, away from Vittorio. As Giudici had heard rumblings of anti-fascist sympathisers at the villa, it's plausible Isa's contact in the *carabinieri* knew something as well. She just had to discover who it was and then turn them in. It wouldn't be too difficult as there are so few people living at the villa – not counting the weekend guests, of course."

Pixley slapped his leg. "That's why Daria was being so helpful with the local police. She probably thought it would divert suspicion elsewhere."

Lord Mayhew continued as if he hadn't heard Pixley. "And Vittorio – was he himself was a fascist?"

Silence fell as everyone looked at Isa. Only Emil sniffed, miserable in his chair. The only person who could match his misery was Madam Zora, whose hands were tied with makeshift handcuffs Moretti had fashioned out of a few colourful scarves. It was sadly appropriate, thought Fina.

"It's true. He was a government informant," said Isa quietly. "At least, that's what he told me. Which is exactly why I had no motive to kill him. If I killed him, *carabinieri* would come looking for him, and I would probably be implicated." She sighed. "I'll be honest that it was much easier to implicate Daria than kill Vittorio."

"She's right," said the marchesa. "If she already planned to turn in Daria, why bother with the potential problems that would arise from murder?"

"But what about Daria and Gustavo?" asked Lady Asher. "Wouldn't they have motives to kill Vittorio?"

"We were planning on leaving," said Gustavo.

"Gustavo!" cried the marchesa.

"I'm sorry, Marchesa. We had no other option."

"I say," said Pixley. "Why haven't those chaps – the *carabinieri* – shown up yet? Particularly if Vittorio was a follower of Il Duce?"

"I'm afraid that's confidential, Mr Marsh," said Giudici.

"Confidential my foot," responded Pixley, ever the persistent reporter. "Come on, tell us, Commissario."

"Let's just say we're keeping the necessary authorities informed."

Ruby faced Giudici and gripped her chair.

"Are you, Commissario?"

38

Giudici's light hum stopped. "I'm sorry, Miss Dove. What do you mean?"

"I'll be direct, then. Who are you?"

Fina gasped, along with the rest of the room. Moretti's eyes narrowed, but he had inched away from Giudici.

Giudici chuckled. "You said you're being direct, but your question is still vague. I'm Salvo Giudici, commissioner of the local police. I live in Bellagio. What more do you need to know?"

Ruby marched to Emil's side and whispered in his ear. He nodded.

"Miss Dove, I must protest. I did not give you permission to speak to the prisoner," said Giudici.

"I apologise, but as you will not answer my question, I had to take additional steps. Emil would like to show us something."

Moretti stepped forward. "Please, do show us, Miss Dove."

Giudici opened his mouth, shut it, and smiled. "What would a murder investigation be without theatricality? Lead on, Miss Dove."

"You'll need to remove Emil's handcuffs," said Ruby.

Giudici shook his head but Moretti said, "I will hold him, sir."

The commissario shrugged and lit a cigarette. "Lead on, intrepid Miss Dove."

Emil whispered to Ruby and she led the party into the library. She pulled on a gold wall sconce near the fireplace mantel.

"And now, all will be revealed," said Lord Mayhew in a grave voice.

But he was the first to gasp when a bookshelf next to the mantel slid aside, revealing a dim recess. Moretti handed Ruby a torch and she disappeared inside. She returned with a black, drape-like material. Then she held it up, still standing in the dark doorway.

The skeleton bones glowed.

"That paint is dangerous," said Pixley. "The chap who invented it died a few years ago from radium exposure. But it is delightful, nonetheless."

"What does it mean?" asked Lady Asher, leaning toward Ruby.

Ruby smiled with satisfaction. She held out the costume to Moretti. "Would you smell this costume, Moretti?"

"Smell it? Yes?" His head swivelled around the gathering, looking for confirmation. Everyone nodded. Except Giudici, and Zora, whom Giudici had a firm grip on.

Moretti bent down and wrinkled his nose. "*Dopobarba*. Ah, perfume. No. Aftershave!" he smiled in triumph. Then he frowned and turned to Giudici.

With his one free hand, Giudici patted Moretti on the shoulder. "Don't worry, Moretti. No need for you to tattle on your chief." He sighed. "How did you know, Miss Dove?"

Fina's mouth dropped open and she looked for a chair. They

had already all been taken as everyone sat back to watch the show.

"I first had a hint when you mentioned the four contest winners from the party. How would you know that, especially when you had just arrived? It was possible someone had told you, but unlikely." She paused. "And then, when you caught me in Daria's room, you were different. As if I was about to discover something about you – you had a distinctly sinister look."

"Trick of the lighting, Miss Dove. Happens to the best of us, especially those of us with craggy faces like my own."

"Commissario, how do you explain the scent of your after-shave on the costume, and Miss Dove's comment?" asked Lord Mayhew.

He sighed and held up his hands. "So. It was like this. I heard rumours the marchesa planned to throw a party. A big party!" He smiled in spite of himself. "And I knew if the *carabinieri* heard about it, not only would the marchesa be in – how do you say – hot water, but I would be as well. No parties, you under-stand." He gestured to himself. "But myself, I love *la festa*. I thought I would watch the party and enjoy myself, too."

"That's why you arrived so quickly the next morning," said Fina. "You already knew there had been a so-called accident."

"*Precisamente.* And I had such a charming conversation with you, Gnaga. It was a shame it had to end, but it was especially important as I had won the costume contest! I left in a hurry so I had to leave the costume behind." He began to hum an Italian opera, though Fina could not place the name.

"At least one of us has a legitimate reason to be up to no good," said Pixley. "What's Emil's excuse? How did you know about this room and why in heaven's name did you hide the costume?"

Emil blew his nose, with Moretti's permission. "I read about the Villa Potenza before I arrived. I love architectural history, so

I consume every book on the subject. I discovered the house had secret passages and secret cupboards – not rooms, but cupboards. The book mentioned particularly the cellar passageway and the cupboard in the library."

"Why hide the costume?" asked Fina.

Emil blinked. "I wanted to study it in private."

Looks of horror and shame crossed everyone's faces.

"*Ach, nein.* I mean I wanted to understand its mechanism. The paint – how it works. I found it in the corridor and assumed the skeleton no longer needed it. Why else would she or he leave it there?"

Pixley sighed. "Emil, we can understand that. What we cannot understand is why you needed to hide it – in a secret cupboard of all places!"

He treated them to an impish smile. "I wanted to see the cupboard and, well, I had to hide something else in there, so I thought I would do both. And I had heard, as you said, there might be something dangerous about the paint, so I didn't want it in my room."

"What else did you want to hide in there?" asked Fina.

"Something that would implicate someone important. And the reason I wanted to flee." He looked around. "If Hazel were here, she could collaborate – no, corroborate – my testimony. I leaked the papers to her."

Pixley's eyes gleamed. "So that's why Fina and I saw you in the church that day. But what papers? What leak?"

"Do you all want to know the real reason why I ran away earlier today?"

39

"We'd better make ourselves comfortable," said the marchesa.

"Not too comfortable, Marchesa," said Emil. "For I believe what I have to say concerns you as well."

The marchesa touched her blonde hair, unconcerned, but said nothing.

Emil paced with his hands behind his back, with the permission of Moretti. Unlike Ruby's pacing, Emil would go one way, make a sharp spin around, and march back in a straight line. "I believe in diplomacy. I truly believe in it, but my experiences of the past year have made me question everything.

"I first realised something was odd when I began receiving reports that Italian troops in Ethiopia knew too much about certain important locations of weapons. These were British weapons caches in Sudan. The British have also been worried about Sudanese nationalists, so they've been storing weapons. The Italians took them, and the only way that could have happened, to my mind, was a leak from a British government official. Then a series of other small incidents happened – they only made sense to me because I knew the intricacies of the circumstances." He turned and stared at Lord Mayhew, whose ruddy complexion had deepened again. "I asked Lord Mayhew, without being direct, and quite frankly, acting like a *dummkopf*, about what happened. He dismissed me and said he didn't know anything."

"Then strange things started happening. My wife fell ill, then I fell ill. We recovered, but every time I ate at the embassy or at work, I started to have allergic reactions, particularly in my eyes, such as my eyelids swelling." He turned to Fina. "My doctor started to tell me I had food allergies, which is why I was so careful with food, Miss Aubrey-Havelock."

"So this is all leading to the fact that Lord Mayhew was poisoning you," said Pixley.

"With atropine, is my guess," said Ruby.

Giudici smiled and wagged his finger. "*Bene*, Miss Dove. Very good."

Pixley continued. "But if that's true, why didn't Lord Mayhew just fire you? Why slowly poison you?"

"He wanted to interfere with my mind," said Emil. "Because you see, whatever he was giving me – atropine was probably just one of the drugs – was also making me hallucinate occasionally. Nothing extreme, you understand, but enough to make me paranoid."

Ruby let out a stream of air. "You mean Mayhew was going to say the leaks were coming from you?"

Emil adjusted his thick glasses. "*Natürlich*, Miss Dove. The problem for him – and then for me – the day we arrived, was that I found an incriminating paper I wasn't supposed to find. Remember when those papers flew?"

"Remember, Ruby, when I told you about the folder I saw that read 'Sudan' across the top?" asked Fina.

"And I told you Mayhew made his money in armaments," said Pixley.

"Yes, I figured it had something to do with Emil's disappearance," said Ruby. "Since I knew he wasn't the killer."

"I must apologise to you, Miss Dove," said Emil.

"Why?" Ruby looked genuinely surprised.

"Because I told Lord Mayhew of your reputation, after Iveta told me about you. After you fainted, I'm quite sure he left that poison in your room. That poison packet."

"That would explain it. I knew I fainted from fatigue and dehydration when I arrived, but later, I couldn't understand who would want to poison me. And who had drugged Iveta so she would fall asleep."

Giudici said, "Moretti. We'll need to search Mayhew's room for any sort of liquid or powder you can find. We'll send it all to the laboratory for testing." He turned to Emil. "But why did you run when you did?"

"I didn't know what else to do. I was in such a muddle and I knew it must be only a matter of time before Mayhew killed me or implicated me in some crime! He is so powerful. Even now, I cannot tell what is real and what is his creation."

Mayhew, who had sat silently through these proceedings, rose. "As you can see, madness is in the air today. First that for chap, Sergio, and now my secretary, who already ran away like a lunatic into the snow. Where did he think he would run? It's a sure sign of a madman."

"No it's not," said Lady Asher.

The marchesa looked at Lady Asher. "Are you thinking what I'm thinking?"

Lady Asher nodded. "It's beginning to dawn on me. Mayhew and I – I thought we'd eventually get married. Those scenes you saw between us in the negotiations were all just an act. Mayhew came onto me strong, and I reciprocated, because – well, he was rich. I'm ashamed to say it, but there it is."

"Marilyn!" cried the marchesa. "That's what happened to

me! That's why I agreed to allow him to come here. I had met him before and he had been most odious, but then he turned charming. I'm not sure why, but I suspect it had something to do with the negotiations. I needed the money, too, so I thought what was the harm in a little flirtation?"

"Quite," said Lady Asher. A flicker of sympathy crossed her face, the first Fina had seen since they'd met. "Mayhew wanted me to back him in the negotiations, although his stance on Ethiopia changed from day to day. I did my best to follow suit, but it was most bewildering. If I didn't know better, I'd suspect he was switching allegiances according to how he thought he could make the highest profit. Since he is quite deeply involved in the armaments industry – is that not so, Lloyd?" She raised an eyebrow at him.

Mayhew had turned to face the wall, arms crossed. He refused to speak.

Giudici said, "This is all very fascinating, and we've now tied up every loose end possible, but we still don't know who murdered Vittorio."

As if in answer to his question, they heard shouts coming from the corridor.

40

"He jumped! He jumped!" screamed Hazel.

She ran toward the stairs, but Moretti caught up and held her. "Please, stop, miss. Please."

"But I must see him."

Giudici had already disappeared out the door.

As Hazel pulled her handkerchief from her pocket, a slip of paper fell to the floor. Fina picked it up and was about to hand it back, when she saw it read 'from Sergio'. She unfolded it and read silently, as Pixley and Ruby looked over her shoulder.

Dear Hazel,

I'm sorry it had to end this way and I am even more apologetic I had to fool you, my dear sister. If you're reading this, I decided I could not go on. I could not spend my life in a lunatic asylum for murdering Vittorio.

I'm not crazy, nor have I ever been. Eccentric, yes, but that's true of everyone at Cambridge. The act I put on was all part of my plan, in case I had to fall back on a justification for committing my crime. As you may have guessed, Vittorio was my father. For years, Mum told me he had died and left us penniless. On her deathbed, she told me he was still alive – that he had abandoned us, and even more unforgivable, he had beaten her. Though she begged me not to, I vowed revenge. I researched him with the help of a Cambridge librarian, and soon began to track his movements across Europe. I'd bring him up in casual conversation whenever I could – at weekend parties – to find out anything I could about him. When the marchesa said she was having this party, I arranged to use the negotiations as a ruse because she said she had invited him.

I don't want anyone else implicated for this crime, so I will tell you the facts. I watched him carefully, looking for any opportunity to poison him. I've read up on my poisons, and had a few with me in case different scenarios should arise. When I saw the cut on his jaw from shaving, I knew I could use it to get atropine into his bloodstream. At first, I stole Madam Zora's syringe – that was easy as she told me about it at lunch – but that was too obvious. I thought I'd use it as a blind. I knew how to get the lights to go out, and all I had to do was roll the syringe onstage. I wasn't sure when the poison would take effect, but I was sure it wouldn't take more than an hour, which was when he was going to perform his trick. It was all risky, I realise, but it wasn't hard to put the poison on his mask, especially since he had disappeared for a while. Anyone could have gone into his room to do that. So the syringe was just a red herring.

I knew this would cause the police a lot of confusion because there was so much misdirection and so many possible mistakes a murderer could have made. But I didn't count on Miss Ruby Dove. Please tell her she has nothing to reproach herself for, as this was all my doing. I don't regret it at all.

All I regret is deceiving you.

All my love,
Sergio

FINA SET DOWN her fork and surveyed the restaurant for the first time since they entered. After inhaling her fish risotto, she felt she could finally relax. She admired the handsome couple at the next table, half-murmuring into their red wine glasses and making sheep's eyes at each another.

"Ripping meal," sighed Pixley.

Ruby pushed back her plate. "I suppose we ought to return to the villa – thank goodness it's our last night there."

Fina nodded and prepared to leave. "Where are my gloves?" she mumbled.

"In your pocket, silly," said Ruby.

"I already looked."

"Did you look in your inside pocket? Remember how you asked the tailor in Milan to make one for you, since you love secret pockets as much as I do?"

"I've had just about enough of secrets as I can stand," sighed Pixley. He finished his brandy and set down the glass. "Cheque, please," he signalled to the waiter.

"Hmmm..." said Fina.

Pixley looked at her and giggled. "Are you thinking what I'm thinking?"

"I believe we all deserve dessert and another round of drinks!"

Ruby grumbled under her breath.

"What's got you in a huff?" asked Pixley. "We know you knew Sergio was the killer."

"But I shouldn't have let it go that far. I'm afraid my need to tie up every loose end got the better of me this time. I should have just said it, and let him react in the moment."

"You weren't to know," said Pixley. "Besides, Sergio was good enough to exonerate you from any blame in the letter."

"True."

"What first put you onto him?" asked Pixley.

"Actually it was you, Pix. When you said how you and your brother looked alike but didn't get along. It set me in the frame of mind of thinking about families, inheritance, and family squabbles. Though it was little to go on at first, I noticed Vittorio and Sergio both had this devilish smile – Giudici's sinister grin reminded me of it. They both had brown eyes—"

"That's not enough, even for you," said Fina.

"No, that's not enough. But their eyes wrinkled in the same way when they smiled. Not everyone has that. And at the ball, Sergio referred to Vittorio as 'the old man'."

"That struck me as odd as well," said Pixley. "I didn't know who he was talking about."

"So that's why you asked Pixley and I to tell you all we knew about the guests' families that night," said Fina. "And it came out that Sergio had an English mother and an Italian father."

Ruby tapped her teeth, clearly somewhere far away. "Yes... that's why. Vittorio was also quite the ladies' man. It wasn't much to implicate him, but I thought it was worth a try."

"I just wish... I just wish..." sighed Pixley.

"Yes, Pix? Your wish is our command!" said Fina.

Pixley pounded the table. Fortunately, no one looked up as a waiter also dropped his tray at the same moment.

"I just wish I hadn't fallen for Sergio. It's preposterous that I, Pixley Hayford, was canoodling with a murderer."

Ruby gave Fina a quick glance. "So you're not heartbroken – you're angry."

"The blighter led me on with sweet nothings, and I fell for it. And to top it off, he pretended to be mad as a bag of ferrets!"

Ruby put her hand over Pixley's. "I saw his eyes – they do not lie. He was falling in love with you, but you weren't part of his original plan."

"You mean I'm still a bit of crumpet?"

"Of course you are, Pix," put in Fina. "Who could resist your red jumper?"

Pixley nodded and slapped his legs. "You're right. Come on, let's enjoy our last night in Bellagio."

"No dessert for me, but I will have a large scotch," said Ruby.

Fina laughed. "Since when have you taken up scotch?"

"Since now."

"I do have two more questions before we drink the night away. Who locked us in the cellar, forcing us into the tunnel?"

"I think it was simply Gustavo or Daria, being conscientious about locking up," said Ruby.

"And who stole those two interview sheets – the ones belonging to Lady Asher and Madam Zora?"

Ruby held up her hands. "Your guess is as good as mine, but I cannot see why Lady Asher would be worried about it. Madam Zora, however, had a great fear of the police. Understandable, given her background in Ukraine, even if she weren't a thief."

Fina nodded, still rummaging around in her bag and coat. "I found my gloves! You were right, Sherlock Dove. They were inside my coat."

"That's not all." Pixley held up an envelope that had fallen to the floor.

She groaned. "Not more letters! I'll read mine so I can enjoy my tiramisù."

She froze.

"Feens? Red? Are you there?" asked Ruby. "Here, let me read

it." She took the letter, glanced at it and took a large gulp of scotch.

She read aloud:

DEAR FINA AUBREY-HAVELOCK,

You think you're clever, don't you? Well, not as clever as Miss Dove, but only I have the claim of being more clever than her. I asked my good friend Vittorio to lure you back to London, but it seems I haven't succeeded. But we shall meet again. Soon.

PIXLEY TOOK OFF HIS GLASSES. "I hope cleaning my spectacles will help me understand what just happened."

Ruby scanned the room. "Moriarty must have left this during dinner. Where was your coat?"

"I gave it to the waiter. She must have slipped it inside."

"That finally explains who was looking at Pixley through the Napoleon painting. It could have been Vittorio, of course, but what would be the point? It was Moriarty."

"So she was in the villa all along," murmured Fina. They all shivered.

The waiter brought Fina's tiramisù. She took a large fork and plunged it into the ladyfingers. Then she piloted the large piece into her mouth, not caring that she had chocolate on her face. "I'm going to drown my sorrows in tiramisù. I may even order another just to show Moriarty that I don't give a fig about her ridiculous letters. She's all talk."

Then she stood up and yelled. "You're all talk, Moriarty!"

The other diners stared at Fina, dumbfounded. The waiter moved forward. Ruby yanked Fina's sleeve.

Pixley doubled over in laughter. "That's the spirit, Feens! We'll show that cowardly Moriarty."

"Shhh!" said Ruby. "You'll get us killed."

Then she giggled.

"A toast." Pixley raised his scotch.

"To good friends and cowardly enemies!"

The End

If you enjoyed this book, would you leave a review on your favorite platform? It means a great deal to me. Thank you!

With gratitude,
Rose

MORE RUBY & FINA!

I'm looking to you, dear reader, to share your views about this series. Reviews online are wonderful and word of mouth is even better.

If you enjoyed this book, I would be grateful if you spent a few minutes leaving me a review on your favorite reading platform.

Thank you!

ABOUT THE AUTHOR

Rose Donovan is a lifelong devotee of cozy mysteries. *The Ruby Dove Mystery Series* is her first foray into fiction, though she has written numerous non-fiction articles unraveling the mysteries of politics and injustice.

www.rosedonovan.com
rose@rosedonovan.com
Reader Group
Follow me on Bookbub

NOTE ABOUT BRITISH STYLE

Readers fluent in US English may believe words such as "fuelled", "signalled", "hiccough", "fulfil", titbit", "oesophagus", "blinkers", and "practise" are typographical errors in this text. Rest assured this is simply British spelling. There are also other formatting differences in terms of spacing and punctuation, including periods after quotation marks in certain circumstances.

For LaVonne

Copyright © 2019 by Rose Donovan

First published in 2019 by Moon Snail Press

www.rosedonovan.com

All the characters in this book are fictitious, and any resemblance to actual persons living or dead is purely coincidental.

All rights reserved. No part of this book may be reproduced or transmitted in any form or by any means, electronic or mechanical, including photocopying, recording, or by any information storage and retrieval system without the written permission of the publisher, except where permitted by law.

Moon Snail Press

Unceded Duwamish Land

Seattle, Washington